"It is the only solution. I need a wife and an heir. I'll inform Sebastiano and have him make the necessary arrangements."

"No! I haven't agreed to anything. You can't make me do this. I'm leaving and you can't stop me."

Sienna scooted to the other side of the bed, swinging her legs over the side and pushing herself off. But Rafe was already there, standing in front of her like a storm cloud, angry and potent and thunderous. But the hand he put to her face was gentle and warm, and she trembled into his touch.

"Leave and I will bring you back. Run and I will catch you. There is no escaping the truth of this, Sienna. You will marry me. You will become my wife."

She looked up at him, afraid to blink, afraid to breathe, lest she break this spell he'd somehow woven around her. How long he stood there stroking her face, and how long she allowed him to, she didn't know.

"There has to be another way," she whispered.

His hand cupping her jaw, he dipped his face to hers and pressed the barest of kisses to her lips. "There is no other way."

Dear Reader,

Harlequin Presents® is all about passion, power and seduction, oodles of wealth and abundant glamour. This is the series of the rich and the superrich. Private jets, luxury cars and international settings that range from the wildly exotic to the bright lights of the big city! We want to whisk you away to the far corners of the globe and allow you to escape and indulge in a unique world of unforgettable men and passionate romances. There is only one Harlequin Presents®, available all month long. And we promise you the world....

As if this weren't enough, there's more! More of what you love.... Two weeks after the Presents® titles hit the shelves, four Presents® EXTRA titles join them! Presents® EXTRA is selected especially for you—your favorite authors and much-loved themes have been handpicked to create exclusive collections for your reading pleasure. There's another excuse to indulge! Midmonth, there's always a new collection to treasure—you won't want to miss out.

Harlequin Presents®—still the original and the best!

Best wishes,

The Editors

Trish Morey

FORCED WIFE, ROYAL LOVE-CHILD

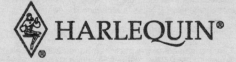

HARLEQUIN®

TORONTO • NEW YORK • LONDON
AMSTERDAM • PARIS • SYDNEY • HAMBURG
STOCKHOLM • ATHENS • TOKYO • MILAN • MADRID
PRAGUE • WARSAW • BUDAPEST • AUCKLAND

Recycling programs
for this product may
not exist in your area.

ISBN-13: 978-0-373-12813-6
ISBN-10:   0-373-12813-4

FORCED WIFE, ROYAL LOVE-CHILD

First North American Publication 2009.

www.eHarlequin.com

Printed in U.S.A.

All about the author...
Trish Morey

TRISH MOREY wrote her first book at age eleven for a children's book-week competition. Entitled *Island Dreamer*, it told the story of an orphaned girl and her life on a small island at the mouth of South Australia's Murray River. *Island Dreamer* also proved to be her first rejection—her entry was disqualified unread and, shattered and broken, she turned to a life where she could combine her love of fiction with her need for creativity—and became a chartered accountant. Life wasn't all dull though, as she embarked on a skydiving course, completing three jumps before deciding that she'd given her fear of heights a run for its money.

Meanwhile, she fell in love and married a handsome guy who cut computer code and later penned her second book—the totally riveting *A Guide to Departmental Budgeting*—whilst working for the New Zealand Treasury.

Back home in Australia after the birth of their second daughter, Trish spied an article saying that Harlequin® was actively seeking new authors. It was one of those "Eureka!" moments—Trish was going to be one of those authors! Eleven years after reading that fateful article (actually on June 18, 2003, at 6:32 p.m!) the magical phone call came and Trish finally realized her dream.

According to Trish, writing and selling a book is a major life achievement that ranks up there with jumping out of an airplane and motherhood. All three take commitment, determination and sheer guts, but the effort is so very, very worthwhile.

Trish now lives with her husband and four young daughters in a special part of South Australia, surrounded by orchards and bushland and visited by the occasional koala and kangaroo.

You can visit Trish at her Web site at www.trishmorey.com or drop her a line at trish@trishmorey.com.

For Gavin, with much love.

Thanks for your endless support over the years, for all the good times and the laughs, and thanks, more than anything, for just being there.

Happy anniversary, honey.

XXX

CHAPTER ONE

THE sex was good.

Surprisingly good.

With a growl Rafe gave himself up to the inevitable and hauled her naked body against his own, drinking deeply of the sleepy scent of her skin, enjoying the way the last remnants of her perfume mingled with the lingering muskiness of passion, and feeling a corresponding tightening in his loins. He'd barely dozed but again he was ready for her and he wasn't about to waste a minute of their first night together. Not after it taking the best part of a week to get her into his bed.

He couldn't remember the last time that had happened.

Through the filmy curtains of his apartment the lights of Paris still glowed, even as the night sky slowly peeled away and the soft light of dawn turned her skin lustrous. He pressed his lips to her neck and suckled at the tender flesh below her ear, and was instantly rewarded with a sound like a purr. His lips curled into a smile on her skin. There was a price for making him wait so long and he'd enjoyed every last minute of exacting his payment.

She stirred into life then, rolling towards him and reaching out, a low sigh vibrating through her as her Titian hair moved across her pillow like a curtain rising on the next act.

How appropriate, he thought, already anticipating it. He raised himself over her, settling between her legs. A week it had taken to get her here. A week they had wasted. He wasn't wasting a moment more.

He lowered his head and captured one ripe nipple between his lips, drawing it in deep, circling the tightening bud with his tongue. She arched under him, made another of those little mewing sounds and clung on, her fingers tangling in his hair.

He loved her breasts, loved their shape and the feel of them in his hands, and he loved the contrast in textures, from their satin-soft skin to their pebbled circles to their bullet-like peaks when she was aroused. Loved making them so. She tasted of woman and salt and sex and he couldn't get enough. And when she lifted her hips and teased her curls against the throbbing length of him, he couldn't see the point of waiting any longer.

Rearing up, he grabbed a packet from the side table, jammed it between his teeth and reefed off the top.

'Let me,' she said, a raw huskiness edging her voice, and a hunger in her hazel eyes that reflected his own desperate need fed into it and ramped it up tenfold. He allowed himself a smile as she took it from him, lifting herself higher on the bed and applying it almost reverentially. He raised his eyes to the ceiling at that first, delicate touch. So much for the woman who just last night had seemed almost nervous about sex. The prospect of the next few weeks was looking better all the time.

And then anticipation turned to agony, his smile morphing into a grimace when she took her own sweet time rolling the damn thing on. He grabbed her hand, finished the job and pushed her down in one fell movement, her gasp of surprise changing to one of delight as he plunged deep into her exquisite depths.

The act of fusion shorted his thought processes, until there was room for just one spark of awareness, barely a thought, more an acknowledgement that seeped through his sex-fogged senses.

Not just good.

The sex was perfect.

That couldn't be her face in the mirror. Sienna Wainwright stopped dead in her tracks and looked hard. The stranger stared back at her, wide-eyed despite the lack of sleep, her lips plump and pink from his attention, and her usually restrained hair coiled and wild with abandon. She looked wanton, thoroughly ravished and a million miles away from who Sienna Wainwright was supposed to be.

Had been!

Until last night. Until the final unravelling of her defences.

Tentatively, almost experimentally, she put the fingers of one hand to her lips, felt their still tender flesh, traced the now blurred line where they melded into the rest of her face.

Rafe had touched her like this, the pads of his fingers tender on her skin, tracing every line and curve of her lips, almost as if worshipping them, before he'd dipped his mouth and kissed her. Kissed her so sweetly it had taken her breath away. Kissed her so passionately it had made her forget all about the insanity of letting him have his way with her.

And before she'd let him have his way with her all over again.

She squeezed her eyes shut and dragged in a breath, her breathing coming in short bursts with the fresh memories of his amazing lovemaking still sparking off thrills in her body like tiny aftershocks.

Rafe Lombardi, international financier and self-made billionaire, and no wonder, given his knack for pulling back businesses from the brink of failure and turning them into global success stories—only the most marriageable and least-attainable man on earth, if you believed what gossip rags world-wide suggested. Sienna had had no reason to disbelieve them or the reports of the long list of one-time partners left shipwrecked in his wake. It was half the reason she'd wanted to keep her distance, if not run a mile in the opposite direction.

She wasn't in Rafe's league and she knew it, economically, socially or sexually, her experience with men up until now limited and frankly disappointing in the bedroom department.

Whereas Rafe Lombardi moved in the highest circles, mixing with the crème de la crème of society, power brokers and tycoons and with the designer women who clung to them like accessories. What would a man like him see in her, a woman who had to work for her living and so far down the social scale as not to register, other than just another chance encounter, another notch in his belt?

So she'd tried to hold him off as long as she could, thinking he'd give up and move on to greener pastures. Expecting he would as soon as she'd told him no the first time.

But he hadn't. Instead of abandoning the chase, he'd pursued her with a single-minded determination that had simultaneously terrified and secretly thrilled her.

Rafe Lombardi was clearly a man used to getting his own way.

She turned on the shower and adjusted the temperature, stepping in and turning her face into the spray, eyes closed as the liquid massage worked its magic on her newly sensitised skin, caressing places where just so recently Rafe had worked his own unique brand of magic and where he no doubt would again as soon as he kept his promise to join her in the shower.

Her body hummed in anticipation. Rafe, that body and water. That would make for one lethal combination.

A bubble of laughter welled up unexpectedly. She'd turned him down how many times these last few days? She must have been mad. For it was clear after just one night with him that any woman in her right senses would take Rafe Lombardi and whatever he offered and hang onto him as long as she possibly could, and to hell with the consequences.

Besides, she'd been working hard these few months, getting herself established back in Europe, with a new home and a new job. She deserved a bit of rest and recreation.

There would be consequences, nothing surer, but for now she hugged the knowledge that he'd asked to see her again like a secret treasure.

She spun around, letting the water pound the back of her neck as she soaped her hair, half a mind anticipating his arrival, the other half employed on working out what it was that made him so different to every other man she'd ever met. His tall, dark good looks, the designer stubble and thick wavy hair that coiled at his collar just a shade too long to be considered conservative were enough in themselves to set him apart from the crowd.

But he was so much more than the superficial. There was a confidence in the way he carried himself and in the masterful way he handled people and situations. He wore power as easily as he wore the clothes on his hard-wired body, and it had terrified her to feel that power, and to know it had been directed one hundred per cent towards her.

She shivered despite the warm torrent, remembering how vulnerable he'd made her feel with just one heated glance, one seemingly innocent brush of skin against skin. He had the gift of making a woman feel so desirable, of making her feel she was the centre of his existence and he'd used that gift mercilessly to flatter her during his pursuit, while his eyes had held a look that somehow seemed to burn its way into her soul and beyond.

And then he'd used that gift to wield her to his purpose in his bed.

She directed her face into the spray on a sigh. No, Rafe

Lombardi was like no man she'd ever met before. Little wonder he'd left a trail of broken hearts in his wake, because if a woman wasn't careful, he was everything that a woman could so easily fall in love with…

Oh, no!

She snapped off the tap and yanked the towel from the rail with a determined flick, angry with herself for letting her thoughts drift so far. Remembering how he'd made her feel, recalling the hungry look in his eye while he remained poised over her in that exquisite moment before their union, that was one thing. But building some fairy tale happy ending that could never happen…

Living in Paris must be going to her head. She'd just landed the job of her dreams. An affair was good. An affair was welcome. She wasn't looking for anything more.

Sienna wrapped herself in a towel, half aware that now the shower was turned off she could hear the sound of the news channel drifting in from the room outside. Rafe had turned it on to check the global money market report before joining her. Which he hadn't. Proof, if she'd really needed it, that she was nothing more to him than a distraction from his high-powered life.

Albeit a distraction he wanted to see again, just a few short hours away. Right now that was enough.

Her hair wrapped turban style under a towel and wearing one of the plush robes she'd found hanging behind the bathroom door, she emerged from the fog-filled en suite. There was a trolley in the room that hadn't been there before from which emanated the tantalising scent of fresh coffee and warm pastries, but Rafe was still standing near the storm-tossed bed where she'd left him, though at some stage he'd pulled on a pair of jeans that hung low on his hips, zipped but with the top button still undone. The sight was nearly enough to bring her undone, until she caught the scowl turning his face to thunder as he listened intently to the stream of frenzied Italian issuing from the television.

She moved closer, and, for the first time since they'd been together, he didn't turn towards her, didn't greet her with that soul-deep smile. After enjoying his almost instinctive reaction to her presence for the past week, she missed it more than she'd expected.

'What is it?' she asked, coming alongside, trying to follow the torrent of Italian delivered too fast for her scant knowledge of the spoken language and, at the same time, unable to resist touching one hand to the small of his back. 'What's going on?'

He silenced her with a hiss, shrugging away from the gesture, away from her, and she sensed distance opening up between them where once there had been none. She heard a name—Montvelatte—recognising it as a tiny principality strategically perched in the territorial waters between France and Italy, and saw a reporter against a shifting backdrop— what looked like a fairy-tale palace lit up against the night sky, then the line of famous casinos fringing the harbour and a picture of the former Prince Eduardo. The reporter continued talking animatedly, accompanying footage of an army of maroon-jacketed gendarmes frogmarching the young Prince and his brother into cars before being driven away from the palace. She frowned, trying to make sense of it all. Clearly something was very wrong in Montvelatte.

The reporter ended his report with a scowl and an emphatic slash of one hand accompanying the words—'"Montvelatte, *finito*!"'

The news programme crossed back to their studio before moving on to their next story. Rafe hit the remote, the screen went black and he turned his back on both the screen and her, raking his fingers through his hair.

She loosened the towel at her hair, began rubbing it in cautious circles, sensing that something major had transpired and knowing she was missing more than what had been reported in the sensational yet indecipherable television coverage.

'What's happening? It looked like the police were carting away the entire royal family.'

He spun round, his ruggedly beautiful face reduced to a mask of tightly drawn flesh over bones suddenly lying too close to the surface, his eyes both wild and filled with something that looked like grief.

'It's over,' he said, in a voice that turned her cold. Then his eyes glazed even colder. 'It's over.'

An inexplicable fear zipped down her spine. Finally he'd acknowledged her presence and yet she doubted he'd even seen her. Right now it was more as if he was looking right through her.

'What's over? What is it that's happened?'

For a minute she wasn't even sure he'd even heard her, his only movement the rapid rise and fall of his chest, but then his chin jerked up and his eyes took on a predatory gleam, finding a focus that had been lacking before.

'Justice,' he said cryptically, crossing the carpet silently in his bare feet until he stood before her, his turmoil-filled eyes holding hers hostage, his naked chest so close it took her breath away. And before she could ask him what he meant, before she could ask what any of it meant, he reached over and took the damp towel from her hands, tossing it purposefully to one side.

Sienna trembled, her pulse quickening as it always did when she had one hundred per cent of his attention, his scent and his aura wrapping around her and pulling her in.

'Tell me,' she whispered in spite of it, refusing to give herself up to his power, knowing that once he touched her, she'd be lost. 'What does it mean?'

Rafe said nothing. Instead, there was a tug at her waist followed by a loosening, and then the sides of her gown fell open. She felt the kiss of air against her skin, heard the hiss of breath through his teeth as he gazed down at the ribbon of exposed flesh, and felt that searing heat of his eyes like the brand of a torch. 'It means I want you,' he said, reaching out the fingers of one hand to scoop back the robe on one side, tracing a path down her aching breast to her nipple and circling that sensitive peak. *'Now!'*

Her body was ready, the swell of her breasts and the insistent thrumming of the pulse between her thighs telling her so. But something flashed across his eyes, and she sensed something of the torment he was feeling, and panic shimmied up her spine as she recognised the truth. He didn't see her at all, not really. She was merely a vessel, a vehicle for release from whatever demons were plaguing him, and once again, she wondered why he seemed to care so much about a tiny island principality that featured in the tabloids more for the exploits of its young Princes and their latest love interests, rather than for any financial concern Rafe would normally be interested in.

Sienna put her hands to his chest, made a move to push herself away. 'I don't know if this is such a good idea,' she warned, her head shaking even though the rest of her body betrayed her by trembling under his skilled hands, and her hands refused to lift from the wall of his chest. 'I have to get to work. I'll be late.'

'Then be late!' he growled, uncaring, before sliding a hand around her neck and pulling her to him. His lips captured hers, punishing and demanding, in a kiss in which it was impossible not to feel the turmoil that held him hostage. He tasted of coffee and need and passion—all these things she had tasted before. But now she tasted something new, something triggered by the news report that drove him, an aching fury that moved his kiss beyond mere passion to something dark and dangerous and all-consuming.

And meanwhile his mouth was everywhere—on her lips, at her throat, on her breasts, hungry as he grappled with her robe, reefing it over her shoulders, forcing it down and pulling her naked body against his. She went willingly then, melting into him because she had no real choice, her senses overloaded with the taste and scent of him, the mouth suckling and nipping at her breast, the brush of denim against her legs, the feel of his hot flesh melting her bones, the sound of his zip coming undone...

So many sensations, building one upon the other, a frenzy of feeling that threatened to consume her whole. And then he was lifting her, urging her legs around his waist, only to lower her slowly down until she felt his rock-hard length nudge at her core, and it was her turn to consume him.

He made a sound as he filled her, harsh like the cry of a wounded animal, as if it had been torn from his soul, and she clung to him, afraid for him.

Afraid for herself.

And then he was pumping into her, so fast and furious that sensation exploded inside her like a fireball. She was falling then, his arms still locked around her, barely aware of what was happening when her back met the rumpled bed and he lifted himself, easing out of her until he sat poised there, at the very brink. Through eyes still blurred with passion she looked up at him, looked into his wild eyes and saw the agony that marked his beautiful face and read the words inscribed on her soul—*it was already too late*—when with a roar he thrust into her, burying himself to the hilt again and again in a final turbulent release that sent her shuddering into the abyss once more.

* * *

It was his voice that brought her back to life, the low, urgent tones as he spoke into the phone rumbling through her like a passing thundercloud, but it was a glance at the clock that catapulted her to full consciousness and back into the bathroom to dress.

He barely noticed her go, his attention almost one hundred per cent on the words his business partner was saying. Yannis Markides, one of the few people on the planet who knew the truth of Rafe's background and the identity of his father, knew more than anyone what the television reports would mean to him.

'You have to go,' Yannis urged. 'It's your duty.'

'Now you're sounding just like Sebastiano. He's already in Paris, apparently, and on his way. He certainly didn't waste any time hunting me down.'

'Sebastiano's right to do so. Without you, Montvelatte will cease to exist. Do you want to be responsible for that?'

'I'm not the only one. There's Marietta too—'

'And the day you drop something like this on the shoulders of your little sister, is the day you lose me as a friend. Anyway, you know law dictates it must be a male heir. This is your call, Raphael, your duty.'

'Even if I go, there's no guarantee I can save it. The island is a financial basket case. You heard the reports—Carlo and Roberto and their cronies have drained the economy dry.'

There was a deep laugh at the end of the line. 'And this isn't what you and I do for a living every day? Bring the fiscally dead back to life?'

'Then *you* go, if you're so concerned. I like my life just the way it is.' It was the truth. He'd worked hard to get where he was, taking on the hardest projects out there and proving to himself time and again he was up to the task. And he'd proven something else to himself—that he didn't need to be royalty to be someone.

'But it's not up to me, Rafe. You're the son, the next in line. There is nobody else who can do what you have to do.' There was a pause. 'Besides, don't you think it's what your mother would have wanted you to do?'

Rafe should have known Yannis would hit below the belt. They'd grown up so close he was better than any brother could ever be. The downside was he also knew how to hit hard and to hit where it hurt the most. He wasn't about to admit that fact, though he couldn't deny another truth. 'I'm just glad she died before she found out his death had been organised by his own sons.'

'Not all of his sons,' Yannis corrected. 'There's still you.'

He laughed, short and hard. 'That's right. The bastard son. The son he exiled along with his bastard's mother and baby sister. Why should I go back to bail out his island nation? It's sickening what happened to him, sickening that his own sons conspired against him. But why should I be the one to pick up the pieces? I hate what happened to him, but I don't owe him a thing.'

'Why should you be the one? Because Montvelattian blood flows in your veins. This is your birthright, Rafe. Seize it. If not for your father's sake, then for your mother's.'

Rafe shook his head, trying to clear his thoughts. Yannis knew him too well, knew he felt no loyalty for a father who had never been more than a name to him, and who had discarded his own son and the woman who had borne him as easily as if he'd been brushing lint off his jacket. Even the knowledge that his death had not been an accident didn't cause Rafe any pangs of loss. It was impossible to lose something you'd never had, and Prince Eduardo had never been part of his life.

But his mother was a different matter. Louisa had loved Montvelatte and had talked endlessly of scented orange groves, of colourful vines, of herb bushes tangy with the spray of sea, and of mountainsides covered with flowers amidst the olive trees that she would never see again.

She'd never forgotten the small island nation that had been her home for twenty-one years and that had spat her out, sending her into exile for the rest of her too short existence.

Yannis was right. It had always been her dream to return. It had never happened in her lifetime, but maybe this was his chance to make it happen for her in spirit.

Merda!

Sienna emerged from the bathroom ready for work and wearing a frown. They'd made love so quickly—too quickly for either of them to have given a thought about protection. The risks of pregnancy were low, it was late in her cycle, but there were still risks and she couldn't help but regret her decision not to renew her prescription for the pill when her course had expired last month. At the time there hadn't seemed much point and finding a new doctor with everything else going on had been the last thing on her mind. She now wished she'd thought about it.

And at the risk of making her even later for work, she couldn't leave without at least broaching the subject.

'We need to talk,' she said, registering that he'd finished the call as she gathered up the last of her things and stashed them in her bag. She turned when he didn't respond. He was still sitting on the bed with his back to her, his head in his hands, a picture of such utter desolation that she would never have recognised him if she hadn't known it was him. His air of authority was gone. His power gone. Instead he wore a cloak of vulnerability so heavy that she felt the weight of it herself. 'What is it?' she asked, drawing closer but afraid to touch him, afraid she might feel the pain that was torturing him. 'What's wrong? Is this about that news report, about Montvelatte?'

For heavy seconds he didn't move, didn't speak—then finally let out his breath in a rush as he lifted his head, his fingers working hard at his temples.

'What do you know of the island?' Rafe asked, without looking around.

Sienna shrugged, thrown by the question. But at least he was talking to her and she knew that the pain would be lesser if he did. She rounded the bed and knelt alongside him on the dishevelled linen, finally game to put a hand to him, sliding her hands over his shoulders, feeling the tension tight and knotted under her fingers, trying to massage it away with the stroke of her thumbs. 'What does anyone know? Other than it's a small island in the Mediterranean, famous for both its stunning scenery and the string of casinos that have made it rich. A Mecca for tourists and gamblers alike.'

He snorted dismissively and twisted then, capturing one hand in his and pulling it to his mouth and pressing it to his lips. Hardly a kiss—his fingers were so tight around hers they hurt, his dark eyes almost black. 'And for gangsters, it turns out. Apparently they've been laundering drug money through the casinos ever since Prince Carlo took the crown five years ago.'

Behind him the clock continued to advance and she cursed inwardly. She had to get to work. It had taken some doing to land the job with Sapphire Blue Charter, only her ability to speak French and three superb references winning her the contract and making up for her being a woman, and an Australian to boot, but she was still under probation. The way she was going this morning she'd be lucky if she still had a job by the time she got to the airport. But she couldn't leave him, not like this. 'It still doesn't make sense. They've arrested the Prince and his brother in front of the entire world's media over unproven money-laundering charges? Whatever happened to being innocent until proven guilty?'

Rafe swept from the bed then, grabbing his jeans, quickly dropping those in favour of a snow-white robe that he wrapped and lashed around himself and that showed his olive skin and dark features to perfection. Through the vast expanse of window behind him it seemed the entire city of Paris was laid out like a glorious offering, the Eiffel Tower the centre-point in a brand new morning, but it was the fiery glare from his eyes that demanded her full attention.

'I didn't say they'd been arrested over the money-laundering charges.'

'Then why?'

'Because now they've been linked to the death of the former Prince.'

For a moment she was shocked into silence, her mind busy recalling the history she knew of the tiny principality. 'But Prince Eduardo drowned. He fell from his yacht.'

His hand dropped away, and his face looked even harsher then, if it were possible, his skin drawn so tight it made her jaw ache in sympathy. 'The authorities have just uncovered fresh evidence. He didn't fall.'

Shock punched into her more effectively than any fist. *'They killed their own father?'* No wonder the news reports were full of it. It was more than a scandal. It was a monarchy in crisis, a diplomatic nightmare. A nightmare that somehow held Rafe in its thrall.

'I still don't understand, though. It's horrible, but why does it matter so much to you?'

Sienna searched his eyes, dark eyes filled with grief and torment and pain that scarred their depths, and saw the shutters come down again even as he moved away from her. But the intention was clear. He'd said all that he was going to say.

A final look at the clock told her she couldn't wait any longer. 'I'm sorry, Rafe, but I really have to go.'

He didn't even turn around. 'Yes.'

She slipped on her shoes, picked up her jacket. 'I don't finish until six tonight. How about I call you once I'm home?'

This time he did look at her and she glimpsed something skate across his eyes, something warm and maybe a little sad. Then he blinked and whatever she'd seen was gone. 'No,' he clipped, 'I can't see you tonight.'

'Oh.' She swallowed, trying desperately not to show on her face how disappointed she felt. 'I've got a late shift tomorrow, but how about Wednesday, then?'

But he just gave a toss of his head and opened a closet door, pulling out a travel bag. 'No. Not then. I'll be away.'

'You're leaving?'

His eyes, when they turned on her, were cold, unfathomable. 'Like I said. It's over.'

And mere disappointment curdled into despair, leaving her feeling wrong and suddenly shaky inside her gut. Hadn't he been talking about Montvelatte when he'd said that? 'Where are you going?'

'Away.'

Crazy. She should have accepted his response for the dismissal it was intended to be—no doubt would have if she had been thinking rationally. But right now she felt crazy. He'd pursued her for a week for the sake of just one night? She'd known she would never be more than a short-term distraction for him and could live with that, but, damn it, she wasn't prepared to let it end just yet, not when such a short time ago he hadn't so much as asked her, but *told* her he would see her again.

'I don't understand.'

'I thought you were late for work!' He tossed the words roughly over his shoulder, not even bothering to look at her as he dragged things from his closet.

Breath snagged in her chest. In another life she would have already left, his dismissal of her more than plain. But not now. Not after the night they'd shared, and when he'd been the one to promise more. 'Is this something to do with that news report, because until that happened, you seemed quite happy to meet up with me again? Why is it that what happens on a tiny island in the Mediterranean is so important to you anyway?'

He stopped pulling things out of the wardrobe then and swivelled around, dumping underwear and shirts carelessly into his carry on as he fired her question right back at her. 'Why is it so important to me?'

And for just a moment, when she saw the pain etched in lines upon his face, she wished she'd never asked. 'You saw those two being carted away by the police.'

'Prince Carlo and Prince Roberto? Yes, of course. What's wrong? Do you know them?'

'You could say that.' A shadow moved across his features. 'We shared the same father.'

Then the buzzer rang and he brushed past her shell-shocked form to answer it. 'I'm sorry, but you really have to go.'

Rafe pulled the door open. 'Come in, Sebastiano,' he said, ushering in an officious-looking man in a double-breasted suit. In the same breath she was ushered out without so much as a goodbye. 'It's been a long time.'

The door closed behind her with a determined click but not before she'd heard the words the older gentleman had uttered in greeting, *'Prince Raphael, you must come quickly...'*

CHAPTER TWO

Six weeks later

THE chopper flew out of the sun, past the blade of rock that was Iseo's Pyramid and low over the line where the cliff met the azure sea. For seconds it hovered effortlessly over the helipad before touching gently down. Rafe watched the descent and landing, knowing who was on board and resenting the intrusion even before the *whump whump* of the rotors had settled into a whine of engines.

'Contessa D'Angelo and her daughter, Genevieve, have arrived, Your Highness,' his *aide-de-camp* announced, appearing from nowhere with his usual brisk efficiency.

'So I gathered,' Rafe answered drily, without putting down the Treasury papers he'd been reading or making any other move to respond. 'I think I'll take that second cup of coffee now, Sebastiano.' He noticed the telltale tic of disapproval in the older man's cheek even as he complied by pouring a stream of rich black liquid from the silver coffee jug into his cup. So be it. If Sebastiano was so concerned with finding a suitable princess for Montvelatte, he could perform the meet and greets himself. After something like half a dozen potential brides in ten days, Rafe was over it. Besides, he had more important issues on his mind, like solving the principality's immediate cash crisis. Montvelatte might need an heir to ensure the principality's future, but there would be no future for any of them if the dire financial straits his half-brothers had landed them in weren't sorted out and soon.

Sebastiano hovered impatiently while Rafe took a sip of the fragrant coffee.

'And your guests, Your Highness? Your driver is waiting.'

Rafe took his time replacing the cup on its saucer before leaning back in his chair. 'Isn't it time we gave up this wife-hunting charade, Sebastiano? I don't think I can bear to meet another pretty young thing and her ambitious stage mother.'

'Genevieve D'Angelo,' he began, sounding suitably put out on the young woman's behalf, 'can hardly be written off as some "pretty young thing". She has an impeccable background and her family have been nobles for centuries. She is eminently qualified for the role as Montvelatte's Princess.'

'And what good is it to be "eminently qualified" if I don't want her?'

'How do you know you don't want her before you've even met her?'

Rafe looked up at the older man, his eyes narrowing. Nobody else could get away with such impertinence. Nobody else would even try. But Sebastiano had been in charge of palace administration for something like forty years, and, while he'd been shunted to one side in his half-brothers' desire to rule unopposed, Rafe credited him with almost certainly being the one thing that had held the principality together during those years of recklessness and financial ineptitude. Not that that meant he had to like what his aide said. 'I haven't wanted one of them yet.'

Sebastiano gave an exasperated sigh, his attention on the recently arrived aircraft. 'We've been through this. Montvelatte needs an heir. How are you to achieve this without a wife? We are simply trying to expedite the process.'

'By turning this island into some kind of ghastly reality game show?'

Sebastiano gave up the fight with a small bow. 'I'll inform the Contessa and her daughter you'll meet them in the library after they've freshened up.' Without waiting for a reply he withdrew as briskly as he'd arrived. Scant seconds later Rafe noticed the golf buggy used to transport travellers between the helipad and the palace heading out along the narrow path.

Rafe sighed. He knew Sebastiano was right, that Montvelatte's future was insecure without another generation of Lombardis, and that nobody would invest the necessary funds in Montvelatte's financial reconstruction without a guarantee of the longevity of the island's status as a principality. But he still didn't like the implications.

The buggy came to a halt alongside the helicopter where his aide emerged crisp and dapper, stooping under the still-circling blades as he approached before opening the door.

Rafe turned back to his papers and the problem at hand. He had no interest in its passengers: the hopeful mother, the 'eminently qualified' daughter. He'd seen the stills, he'd seen the tapes and the two-minute interview, all of which had been provided to give him the opportunity to assess how this particular marriage prospect looked, walked and talked and how she might satisfy at least half the requirements of a future Princess of Montvelatte—that of looking the part. The other half—*doing her part*—had been apparently already assured by a barrage of eminent medical specialists.

Rafe had no sympathy for these women, these carefully selected marriage prospects, who seemed so keen for the opportunity to parade in front of him like some choice cut of meat. All so they might secure marriage to a near perfect stranger and, through it, the title of princess.

It made no sense to him. What they had subjected themselves to to prove that their families and their past were beyond reproach and that there were no health impediments to both conceiving a child and carrying it to full term, beggared belief.

On the other hand, nobody had dared question his prowess to conceive a child, for despite the scandalous circumstances of his own bastard birth thirty-three years ago, he had the right bloodlines and that, it was deemed, was sufficient.

He would have laughed, if it weren't the truth. A hitherto unknown prince had appeared on the scene in a blaze of publicity and suddenly everyone wanted a piece of the fairy tale.

Rafe glanced up, noticing Sebastiano's lips move as he handed the second of the women into the buggy, the silky outfit she was wearing shifting on the breeze, rippling like the sea.

Even from here he could see she was beautiful. Tall, willow slim and every bit as elegant as the photographs and film footage suggested.

But then they were all beautiful.

And he was completely unmoved.

He sighed. Maybe that was one good thing about this search for a princess. At least nobody would labour under the misapprehension that this was a love match. At least he would be spared that.

The woman hesitated a fraction before entering the vehicle and turned her silver-blonde head up towards the palace, scanning from behind her designer sunglasses. Was she looking for him, wondering where he was and whether the snub of not being there to greet her was deliberate? Or was she merely sizing up the real estate?

Rafe drained the last of the thick, rich coffee and collected his papers together. He would have to meet her, he supposed.

He might as well get it over with. But he would talk to Sebastiano and make him see sense. This system of princess hunting that Sebastiano and his team of courtiers had devised was no basis for a marriage. Especially not his.

Over at the helipad the buggy's cargo was safely loaded, and the buggy was pulling away when the door of the helicopter was thrown open and the pilot jumped out, running out after the vehicle with a small case in his hands.

And it hit Rafe with all the force of a body blow.

Not *his* hands.

Her hands!

He was on his feet and at the terrace balustrade in an instant, peering harder, squinting against the glare of the sun. It couldn't be…

But the pilot was definitely a woman, a tight waist and the curve of her hip accentuated by the slim-fitting overalls, and, while sunglasses hid her eyes, her pale skin and the copper-red hair framing her face were both achingly familiar. Then she turned after delivering the bag and a long braid slapped back and forth across her back as though it were a living thing.

Christo!

He pounced on the nearest phone, barking out his first ever order to the Palace Guard, 'Don't let that helicopter go!'

Sienna had to get out of here. Her knees were jelly with relief that Rafe hadn't been there to meet the helicopter, her stomach churned and if she didn't get off this island in the next thirty seconds she was going to explode. Although, the way her insides felt after that panicked dash to deliver her passenger's forgotten bag, she might just explode anyway.

Sienna sucked in a deep, and what she hoped was a calming, breath and with clammy hands pulled the door of the chopper shut, clipping on her headset. Thinking he might be there when she landed—dreading it—had put her in a cold sweat the entire flight.

And she was still sweating. It didn't help that it was so hot today, especially out here on this rocky headland, where the effect of the hot Mediterranean sun was compounded by the way it bounced off the white painted walls that coiled along the narrow road up to the castle like a ribbon. And the castle up the top—the fairy-tale castle that rose out of the rock, ancient and weather-worn and beautiful, the fairy-tale castle now presided over by Prince Raphael, last of the long and illustrious line of Lombardi.

Prince Raphael. Oh, my God, she'd slept with a prince. *Royalty.* And she'd had no idea. But nobody had back then. It had only been in the days after he'd practically tossed her out of his room that the news of the discovery of a new-found prince for Montvelatte had broken. Sensational news that had rivalled the earlier news of the downfall of the then incumbent and his brother.

And it had seemed as if every newspaper, every magazine and every television programme had been full of the news, digging into the once buried past, and uncovering the story of the young nanny who'd become the Prince's lover, only to be exiled with a young son and another baby on the way. The coronation that had followed had kept the story alive for weeks.

And his face had been everywhere she'd looked, so there was no hope of forgetting him during the day, no chance of escaping the face that haunted her in her dreams.

He was a prince!

No wonder he'd changed his mind about seeing her again. He would have known what that news report had meant—that he'd have even less reason to slum it with the likes of her.

Why would he, when he clearly had his pick of society's brightest and prettiest? There'd been a constant stream of women being brought to the island in the past few days. Nothing had been said at the base—they knew that discretion was the better part of business success—but she knew from personal experience. Prince Raphael was a man of big appetites…

Her stomach churned, the taste of bile bitter in her mouth as she completed the preflight checklist. The sooner she was away from this island and the sooner there was no risk she would run into the man who'd so unceremoniously thrown her out of his life, then the sooner this damned queasiness would settle down. Ever since she'd been told she'd been rostered on for this assignment she'd felt physically ill. Montvelatte was the last place on earth she wanted to be. Knowing she'd just delivered his latest love interest made it doubly so.

Sienna yanked herself back from that thought with a mental slap to the head.

What was she thinking? Genevieve, or whatever her name was, was welcome to him. She was out of here.

There was the roar of another engine, the blast of horns and she turned to see a jeep screeching to a halt alongside the helipad in a spray of gravel and dust, and the churning in her gut took a turn for the worst. It didn't get any better when four uniformed officers jumped out, gesturing to her to cut the rotors. This was supposed to be a simple drop-and-run. Surely there was no obscure paperwork she'd forgotten to complete?

She was making a move to open the door when it was pulled open for her from the other side. The officer saluted so properly that even over her own thumping heartbeat, Sienna imagined she could hear the snap of his heels clicking together. She'd seen that uniform before—in the footage of the former Prince and his brother being carted away—and she wasn't at all sure that was a comforting thought.

'Signorina Wainwright?'

Breath caught in Sienna's lungs and gave birth to a new strain of fear. *They knew her name?*

She shook her head, removing her headset once again. 'Y-yes,' she stammered. 'Is there a problem?'

'There is no problem, I assure you,' the officer told her in his richly accented English. 'Please, if you would just step outside the aircraft,' he added, offering her his hand to alight the helicopter. His words and actions were accompanied with a smile so seemingly genuine that for a moment she thought everything must be fine after all, that her most recent panic attack was unwarranted and that this was merely some kind of quaint formality nobody had thought to warn her about.

But once outside he made it clear that he expected her to keep moving. Towards the jeep.

Sienna stopped, the men either side of her coming to a halt also. 'What's going on?'

'It is but a short trip to the Castello,' he said, neatly side-stepping her question and throwing her thoughts into turmoil.

Her eyes swung up to the palace that sat atop the massive rock that made up this part of the island. It stared down at her with its thousand window eyes, and for the first time she didn't notice the beauty of the ancient stone architecture with its arched windows and flag-topped turrets, but the thick walls and the fortifications all around that had protected it from invaders for centuries. This time the fairy-tale palace had disappeared, and it was the fortress that she noticed, the fortress she knew instinctively would be just as hard to escape from as to break into.

The fortress that contained the man she least wanted to see in the world.

Oh, no. No way was she going there.

She swallowed back on the sick feeling in a stomach that was once again threatening to unload its pitiful contents at any time, while the hot sun wrung even more perspiration from her nervous body. Her overalls stuck to her in all the wrong places, and sweat beads slid lazily along the loose curling tendrils at her fringe and neck.

'Look, I don't really have time for this. I have to get the chopper back to base. They're expecting me.' She cast a desperate look back over her shoulder towards the helicopter, frowning when she noticed that the remaining two officers had taken up guard duty in front of the chopper, strategically placing themselves between her and the door and effectively cutting off that means of escape. Even if she could have outrun these two beside her.

'Please,' the officer urged, gesturing towards the jeep.

Finding what little shred of courage she still had left, she kicked up her chin. 'And if I insist on being allowed to leave? If I refuse to accompany you to the palace?'

He smiled again, but this time it was a little lighter on the charm, a little heavier on the menace. 'In that unfortunate case,' he said, adding a little bow, 'you would leave me with no choice. I would be forced to arrest you.'

CHAPTER THREE

SIENNA had had enough. For almost three hours she'd been stuck inside this drawing room, prowling the walls holding her prisoner like a caged lion at the zoo.

It didn't matter that the drawing room was the size of a small country and that the accoutrements, the Renaissance tapestries gracing the walls, the crystal chandeliers and fine furniture, made it much more pleasant than any zoo enclosure she'd ever seen. Nor did the constant visitors make a shred of difference, bustling in and out and offering her refreshments and any number of pastries or other tasty delights that she desired.

She wasn't about to be taken in by window dressing. The now familiar maroon-clad guards she'd spied perched at their posts outside the door every time they'd opened had made it more than clear that she was not some welcome guest, but a prisoner in a cage, albeit a very gilded one.

And while at first she'd been nervous, anxious about having to confront Rafe again and certain that he must be the one behind her detention, after waiting this long with no information she was beyond nervousness and frustration. She was furious.

Not one person she'd met here—was able to tell her exactly why she was being kept against her will or when she would be allowed to leave.

The bearer of the pastries had waved her questions aside with a sweep of a hand and had seemed insulted she hadn't been more interested in tasting the proffered wares. The tea bearer had pretended he was ignorant of both English and French and had looked benignly down his crooked nose at her when she'd attempted her rudimentary Italian.

She had a helicopter that had been due back at base hours ago and nobody had allowed her anywhere near a phone to let them know she'd been detained. A missing helicopter. A missing pilot with it. And while the fragrant sweet tea had settled her stomach, it would take something a lot stronger, if not a minor miracle, to settle her nerves. Her earlier nausea was nothing to how she felt now. She would lose her job over this for sure.

Then she heard it, the familiar whine of helicopter engines leading up to that *whump whump* of the rotors. And not just any helicopter. In fact, if she didn't know better…

She ran, her heart sinking with every step, to the large arched windows overlooking the helipad in time to see the helicopter rise up and turn to point out to sea.

Her helicopter!

'No!' she cried, slapping her open palm on the window fruitlessly, knowing there was no chance that whoever was flying the craft could see her, but continuing to slam her hand against the glass anyway as the helicopter accelerated away, already shrinking into the distance.

And mere anger turned incendiary.

There were two doors into the room—one she figured led to the kitchens from where the coffee and cakes had issued. She ran instead to the other, the large double doors she'd entered through and that she knew led to the entrance lobby, the same doors that had remained firmly closed against her until now. She pulled with all her weight against their handles, banging on the wood with her closed fists when she found them locked. 'That's my helicopter. Let me out!' When the doors stayed closed, she rattled the handles some more, her fury rising further as they refused to budge. She cursed out loud. Why the hell wouldn't they let her out?

'I know you're out there,' she yelled at the wall of solid wood, punching it some more for good measure. 'I know you can hear me. I demand to see Rafe. Right now. Where is the cowardly bastard?'

'Here in Montvelatte,' came a familiar voice behind her, a voice that sent panic sizzling down her spine like an electric shock, 'the usual form of address is Prince Raphael, or Your Highness, rather than "the cowardly bastard".'

Sienna swung around, vaguely aware of her braid slapping heavily against the timber door, all too aware of the impact of him slamming into her psyche. She'd demanded to see him and yet still she was totally unprepared for the sheer onslaught of this man on her senses.

And standing there, not two metres away from her, it was some onslaught. It was the same Rafe she remembered, but smoother, his thick wavy hair a little shorter and more tamed, his designer stubble smoothed to a mere shadow. But the sheer intensity contained in his eyes packed as much punch as they ever had. *More.* Because those eyes pinned her now, scanning her lazily from the top of her head to the toes of her boots and all points in between, until the skin under her uniform tingled, her nipples tightening to peaks under his continued scrutiny.

She swallowed, her breathing still ragged, her colour still high from her exertions on the door, if the heat she was feeling in her face was any indication, and it occurred to her in that moment the gulf between them had never been wider or more extreme. Because Rafe was now a prince and looked every part of it, so cool and urbane in his fine wool jacket, so groomed and superior, whereas she was still a nobody, and right now a dishevelled and flustered one.

But so what? She didn't give a damn about his title, not after the way she'd been treated. She was little more than a prisoner here. The last thing she would do was grovel.

'I call it like I see it,' she shot back, refusing to apologise for the outburst or the terminology she'd resorted to.

His eyes narrowed, his expression hardening. 'So I noticed. I can see your mood was not improved by the delay. I'm sorry to have kept you waiting so long. I was unavoidably detained.'

'You were detained?' She shook her head in disbelief. 'Who are you trying to kid. It was me who was detained, prevented by your goons from taking off, and threatened with arrest if I didn't go along with their plans. *I'm* the one who's been detained for hours, held here against my will, and now my helicopter's been stolen—'

'It hasn't been stolen.'

'It's gone! Someone's taken it without my permission. I call that stolen.'

'It's been sent back to base. You're not the only one who can fly a helicopter.'

'Oh? And that's supposed to make everything okay? I was due back with that helicopter. Instead I've been locked inside this prison you call a palace. Well, I've had enough. I'm leaving.'

Sienna launched herself across the room, aiming for the door he must have come through, figuring that one at least might still be unlocked, when his hand snaked out and took hold of her forearm, using her momentum to spin her back around.

'You're not going anywhere.'

The words were a whisper but deadly sure in their intent. She looked down at the hand burning a brand into her flesh, then up to his face, and almost wished she hadn't. His eyes, once filled with passion and longing and desire for her, now harsh and flat and so cold that she shivered.

'And if I don't want to stay?'

'You'll stay.'

'Why should I?'

'Because I want you to.'

The unexpected words sounded like they'd been ground through his teeth, their intensity rocking her to the soles of her feet so that she felt herself sway towards him, as if drawn by some invisible thread. Drawing her so close that his masculine scent wrapped around her and drew her even closer. She'd dreamt of such a moment, on countless sleep-elusive nights, and in pointless daydream wishes. Wished it long and hard, even after she'd seen the news reports declaring that Rafe was indeed the new Prince of Montvelatte, and realising it could never be so.

But she was here now... She searched his face, his eyes, looking for the truth, trying to discover what it meant.

And then damned herself for hoping, straightening suddenly, her back once again rigid and set. This was the man who'd thrown her out of his room and his life without so much as a goodbye once before. There was no way she'd give him the chance to do it again.

'And that matters to me because?' She wrenched her arm from his grasp. 'No, thanks. I'm leaving. And if you won't arrange my departure, I'll damn well find a way out of this hellhole myself.'

'You're not leaving.' It wasn't a question. It was a bald statement of fact and it used up the last remaining shred of patience Sienna had.

'Who the hell do you think you are to tell me what I can and cannot do? They make you a prince and suddenly you think you're the ruler of the universe? Well, let me tell you,

Rafe, or Raphael or whatever it is you like to call yourself now, you're not my prince. I didn't vote for you!'

Silence followed her words, so thick and heavy that she wished away the thump of her heart lest he hear it and read too much into it.

She was angry.

Furious.

Nothing more.

And then, totally unexpectedly, he threw back his head and laughed, really laughed, deep and loud. So deep that it was too much and cut her right where it shouldn't hurt and yet still did. So deep that she took advantage of his lack of attention and decided to make good her escape.

She didn't get far.

'Sienna,' he said, as his hands trapped her shoulders and collected her in, pulling her around until she faced him, and holding her close. So close than the room shrank until it was just his scent that surrounded her, coiling into her all over again. So close that she had to shut her eyes to block out the sight of the triangle of skin exposed by the undone-at-the-collar shirt, a patch of skin her mouth knew intimately.

'Let me go,' she protested, squirming in his arms, lashing out at her gaoler while the prick of tears was dangerously close. 'Stop laughing at me!'

'I wasn't laughing at you,' he said, with such conviction that she stopped thrashing about and dared open her eyes. And what they met was a gaze so intense and fathomless that she felt it resonate to the soles of her feet. She watched his eyes drift purposefully southwards, felt their heat on her lips before it was the touch of a finger she felt there. She gasped, her lips parting with the shock of it, and dragged in air laced with the very essence of him. 'Do you know how long it is since I've had someone really disagree with me?'

She wavered, thrown off balance by this sudden change in mood and by the electricity generated by his touch. But only for a moment. She knew what charm the man possessed— hadn't it succeeded in getting her into his bed that first fateful time, even after she'd tried everything she knew to put him off? She couldn't afford to let him through her barriers a second time.

Even so, it took everything she possessed to muster a defence. She stiffened in his arms, determined to be resolute. 'Ten minutes? Fifteen at the outside. Surprise me.'

His smile widened, as if delighted by her response, rather than irritated by it as she'd intended. 'Here I am surrounded by advisers and counsel but not one person has dared to disagree with me since that night I learned I was to become Montvelatte's ruler.' He looked down at her, smoothed a wayward tendril of hair from her brow, the touch of his fingers setting fire to nerve endings under her skin. 'Not until today when you blew back into my life like a breath of fresh air.'

His words flowed like liquid promise through her veins, spreading warmth and hope and all the things she'd missed in these past few weeks, all the things she'd known even back then she had no right to, all the things she had even less right to now. It was exactly the way he'd lured her into their previous affair, by telling her she was different, that she was special. By making her feel special.

And look how that had ended.

Bitterness spiked in her gut, lending her new strength. Sienna shook her head, shrugging off his hand and twisting out of his reach. 'I can imagine how much it must gall you being surrounded by sycophants,' she shot back. 'Now, is there a telephone or some other means of communication I can use to contact my employer and make arrangements for blowing right out of here again?'

To her surprise he let her go this time, and she edged cautiously away, forcing herself not to bolt in case those manacles he called hands locked down on her once again. She skirted the intricately carved lounge suite that held pride of place in the centre of the room in front of a majestic fireplace, all the while scanning the room's contents for a telephone she might have missed earlier, while keeping one eye on Rafe. Making sure he kept his distance. It had taken every last shred of self-control she possessed to tear herself out of his embrace. How long could she keep doing so? How many times could she be constrained by those arms before she stopped fighting altogether and gave herself up to the temptation his body offered, the temptation she had given herself up to once before?

How many times?

What a joke.

How *few* times?

But at least for now he remained where he was, seemingly content to watch her from a distance. If his stance was relaxed and casual, a smile tugging at his lips as he leant back against a polished timber table with his hands at his side on the glossy wood and his ankles crossed in front of him, there was nothing of a smile about his eyes. She shivered, reaching out to clutch the cool wood of the lounge back as she felt their purposefulness wash over her. They were the eyes of a predator, glinting and dangerous, and right now they were fixed on her, content just to watch. She turned away before he might see her fear. The sooner she was out of here and away from Rafe, the better.

Why didn't he make a move to stop her? Did he know the door she was heading for was locked and her quest to escape doomed accordingly? Her already wary footsteps slowed. Was he merely playing with her like a cat with a mouse, letting her think she would soon be free when she was trapped in here until he deigned to let her out? And would he laugh again when she turned the handle of the door to find that, too, locked?

Sienna swallowed back on a gasp that threatened to turn into a sob, tears of frustration all too close.

'It's locked, in case you were wondering,' he said behind her, reading her thoughts and her intentions with ice-cold precision.

She didn't want to believe anything he said but she believed that. Why would he allow her any chance of escape when he'd kept her locked up the entire afternoon?

So she threw him a cold look over her shoulder and changed direction, heading towards the wall of full-length windows instead of towards the door, as if that had been her goal all along. 'I don't know what you're talking about,' she lied.

She came to a halt next to the window, her arms crossed over her thumping chest, thankful that at least she'd managed to put several metres between them as she pretended to gaze out unconcernedly over a view of sea and sun and cliff-top so spectacular it should have taken her breath away.

But it was the empty helipad that filled her vision and thoughts, a sight that tore at her all over again and freshened the sting of unshed tears. How the hell was she supposed to explain what had happened when she got back?

'Why are you so desperate to leave?' Even from across the vast room, his rich voice filled the room like it was little larger than a shoebox. 'I thought we could use a little time to get reacquainted.'

She shot him a look, sending her braid flicking heavily over her shoulder. 'You really expect me to believe you mean re-acquainted? Or horizontal?'

His eyebrows lifted at that one. 'I didn't realise you'd be in such a hurry, but if that's what you'd prefer...'

Her cheeks burned and she turned back towards the glass. Why the hell had she given him any idea of the direction of her thoughts? And the answer came back instantaneously, loud and clear. Because she only had to look at this man and her thoughts turned horizontal, along with her wishes and desires. 'The only hurry I'm in is the hurry to get out of here.'

'You have no desire at all to resume our relationship?'

'We never had a relationship!'

'No? What would you call it, then?'

'A fling. A one-night stand. And I would have thought that given that night is long since over, then so too is any kind of "relationship" we might have shared.'

'You think it's over?'

This time it was her turn to laugh. 'Oh, I think you made that pretty plain at the time.'

She turned, wanting to see his reaction to that but finding him suddenly closer, shocked that she'd been totally unaware that he'd silently closed half the distance between them while she'd kept her gaze fixed sightlessly at the window.

He stopped a few short paces from her, his head tilting, his gaze delving deep into her. 'You're angry with me. Because I let you down.'

'No way!' *That would imply she actually cared one way or the other.* 'I think we both got what we wanted that night. I'm over it.'

'Are you,' he said, one side of his mouth turned up as he moved still closer, 'I wonder.'

She scoffed, and continued to stare pointedly towards the window in an effort to disguise the backward movement of her feet. 'Don't be ridiculous.'

'I think you're afraid of what might happen if you do stay.'

'I'm angry, is what I am.' She lifted her chin defiantly. 'Because you think you can ride roughshod over anyone and everyone.'

'And you wish it could have turned out differently.'

Her shoulders hit something solid and she looked around to find herself wedged in the corner of the room, her frustration mounting as his words struck too close to home and his physical presence came too close for comfort. She backed up tight against the corner, thankful for the solidity of the centuries-old walls. 'Look, does this palace actually have a telephone service? I'm already late back. I really don't want to delay my departure any longer.'

'Stay,' he said, resting one hand up on the wall beside her head with his elbow bent, now so close she had to tilt her head up to meet his eyes. 'Have dinner with me tonight.'

She shook her head, wishing the action would also negate the intoxicating scent of the man that came with his proximity. 'Not a chance. I have to get back and you know it.'

'So get back later. I'm a lonely prince in a *castello*. Indulge me.'

'Indulge you?' She attempted another laugh—there was no way she was feeling sorry for him—but this one came out all brittle and false so she switched to words instead, remembering the precious cargo she'd had to transport to the island only hours earlier. 'Besides, what about your Signorina Genevieve? Won't she be expecting you to dine with her? Or are you planning on abandoning your latest plaything in order to slum it with the hired help?'

His eyes took on a feral gleam. 'My "latest plaything"? Oh, now, that is interesting.'

She regarded him suspiciously, 'What are you talking about?'

'Merely that anyone would think you were jealous. And why would you be jealous of the Signorina Genevieve unless you thought she had access to something you wanted—or perhaps, *someone?*'

'Don't flatter yourself! As far as I'm concerned, she's welcome to you.'

He sighed. 'I'm sure she would be pleased to hear you say that, but, alas, Signorina Genevieve has already departed, courtesy of the helicopter you left so carelessly unattended.' Sienna opened her mouth to protest but he cut her off with the briefest touch of his finger to her lips, a touch which caused a hitch in her breath as her senses sizzled into high alert again. 'Which means I find myself without a dinner companion tonight.' He gave a very stiff bow. 'Would you do me the honour?'

It was surreal. Whatever had transpired between them before, he was now a Mediterranean prince, bowing to a complete nobody and asking her to dine with him.

Unless he was merely desperate…

'So Lady Genevieve turned you down and you expect me to pick up the pieces?'

Rafe's hand slammed against the wall alongside her head, before he spun and strode away, his hands on his hips. And when he turned, it was a flash of fury she saw in his eyes.

'This is nothing to do with Genevieve or anyone else. This is between you and me.'

'Why?' she asked, all too aware of the breathlessness that accompanied her question. 'Why me?'

He moved closer, stopping only inches away before he raised a hand to her face and traced the curve of her jaw. 'Because the moment I saw you emerge from that helicopter, I knew I wanted you again.'

She gasped, heat rushing through her on a tide. His brazen admission shocked her to her core, but already she felt the answering call of her body to his words in the tightening fullness of her breasts and the aching need between her thighs, and she knew without a shadow of a doubt that if she didn't get out of here soon, she would once again fall victim to the sensual spell he cast around her.

'Th-that's too bad,' she stammered. 'I have to go.'

'But that's impossible,' he told her, still in that mellifluous ribbon of a voice, a ribbon that seemed to be drawing ever tighter around her. 'Because you see—' he gestured out the window to where a catamaran could be seen rounding the headland and speeding away from the island '—that's the last vessel to sail to Genoa today. And you've just missed it.'

His words blasted through the sensual fog more effectively than a dousing with a bucket of iced water. She watched the catamaran power into the distance, leaving behind twin trails of foaming water, feeling herself just as churned. 'There has to be another way off! An airport. A private charter—'

'Sadly, not today. And as you can see, we have no helicopter—'

'That's crazy. It's barely six o'clock in the afternoon. There must be something—'

'As I said, not today. Tonight there will be no moon, and Velattians are superstitious; nobody will risk travelling while the Beast of Iseo patrols.'

'What the hell are you talking about?'

'The Beast of Iseo. Surely you've heard of it.' He pointed again out the window to where the massive jagged blade of rock thrust from the sea into the sky some kilometres from the island. 'Iseo's Pyramid, the remnants of the caldera of an ancient volcano, is its home. According to the ancient legend, The Beast of Iseo emerges on the blackest of nights, foraging for wayward travellers. It's a charming legend, full of local colour, don't you think? Although it does mean you will be forced to spend the night here.'

The full impact of what he was saying hit home like a sucker punch. She was trapped here for the night. *With him.*

'I'm not staying here with you. I can't. My employer will be waiting for me. I'll lose my job...'

'Your employer has been made aware of the situation and the fact you will be staying. Besides, you have no choice; there is no way of getting you off the island, even if I could help you.'

'But it makes no sense. It's just a legend. And yet you cease all transport to and from the Island because of it?'

'You're not superstitious, Sienna? You don't believe in the Beast?'

'Oh, I believe in the Beast of Iseo. Right now I'm looking at him.'

He laughed in a way that made it plain he was enjoying his role as captor all too much, and that got so far under her skin that there was no coming out. 'You bastard. You planned all this, didn't you? You kept me here, waiting for hours, knowing I'd be trapped and that I'd have no choice but to stay on the island.'

He shrugged, looking far too smug for her liking. 'I fear you misjudge me. It was hardly my intention at all, merely an unfortunate result of Lady Genevieve's stage mother's inability to accept no for an answer. But maybe her recalcitrance was more fortunate than I gave it credit for.'

He gave another bow, this one a mere shadow of the one he'd given before. 'Now that you have no choice, you might as well accompany me to dinner.'

Sienna shook her head, knowing that way could only result in misery for her, knowing she had to be strong for her pride's, if not her sanity's, sake. 'No, thanks. Not a chance. I'll find a hotel somewhere. I'll stay overnight on the island if I have to, but I will not join you for dinner. Not after everything you've done today.'

One eyebrow raised, he turned a quizzical gaze at her. 'All I've done is to want to spend more time with you.'

'Without asking me? By risking my job? No, thanks. I don't need that kind of intervention. I'll stay at a hotel and leave tomorrow.'

'You have money for this hotel? And for the fare you will surely need? Montvelatte might only be a small island country, but we are not so naïve as to extend credit to anyone who so asks.' His eyes scanned her fitted uniform with the efficiency of an X-ray machine, making her skin prickle under the heavy-duty drill. 'Your outfit is very practical for flying, but I do not see where you might have secreted away so much as a credit card.'

She burned with humiliation, wishing away her body's inevitable reaction to his interest, remembering how once before in just one night that interest had succeeded in turning her from an under-experienced woman into a wanton.

'If you were any kind of gentleman, you'd pick up the expense of my departure, given you've disposed of my means of transport behind my back and without my permission.'

'If I were any kind of gentleman, you would not have found me half as satisfactory in bed...'

His eyes claimed victory; his mouth celebrated it in a smile.

Sienna spun away, her teeth biting into her lower lip as she battled to find a way out of this mess. Of course he wasn't going to offer her the fare out of here. And, of course, she didn't have a purse. All she had on her was her ID, a locker key and a few euros in change. But her purse and credit cards were locked away for safe keeping back at the base, the base she should have returned to hours ago.

Damn him!

'In which case,' he continued, obviously taking her silence as confirmation, 'and seeing I have caused you such distress, I feel it is my duty to offer you accommodation here, in the Palace of Montvelatte. You will find the palace very comfortable, despite its great age.'

She glared up at him, knowing she was beaten but not prepared to show it in her face.

'And I will leave the island tomorrow on the first available transport.' It wasn't a question, and right now if he argued the point there was every chance he would end up an even shorter-lived ruler of Montvelatte than his half-brother.

Once again, he made that nod of assent, almost a bow. 'If that is what you wish.'

She hesitated. Could she trust him? Dared she? But then did she have a choice? 'Then I will stay. Just for tonight. But I will dine in my room.'

His eyes glinted with something unfathomable. 'But of course,' he agreed. 'Now, let me find someone who can show you to your room. I imagine you'd appreciate the chance to freshen up.'

If she needed reminding of the state she must look, she didn't want to hear it. But she followed him across the room, already looking forward to having some breathing space to herself, a room where the air wasn't tainted by the very essence of him on every breath.

It's just one night, she told herself. *Just one night.* Tomorrow he would have to let her go. Tomorrow she would be free.

He reached the door and twisted the handle, pulling it open. 'After you.'

She froze. The door had been unlocked the whole time, the guards she'd seen earlier gone. She'd been just scant feet from the door when she'd decided she'd rather play it cool than be humiliated again. And yet she could have turned the handle and made her escape while he was still a room away. Could she have got away, past the palace guards and the staff? Was there a chance she could have made it to the port in time? She would have managed the fare somehow—offered her watch for collateral—she would have borrowed or begged some form of transport to get herself off the island.

But she hadn't even attempted to leave the room.

And somehow that was the greatest disappointment of all.

CHAPTER FOUR

THE bath was hot and deep, the foaming bath gel forming a mountain of scented bubbles that comforted her body and soothed her fragile soul. Sienna sighed as she slid down into the slippery water, letting her hair fan out around her like a mantilla and gasping as she came back up again, feeling the weight of water streaming from her hair. Heaven. For a centuries-old palace, the plumbing was definitely state of the art and a major improvement on the cantankerous contraption her landlady labelled a shower and which justified her charging fifty percent over the odds for one shoebox of an apartment in the Thirteenth *Arrondissement*.

The best part of an hour later, feeling more relaxed than she had all day, she rinsed off the last of the bubbles and wrapped herself in the large plush towels provided. Marble, gold and mirrors, she thought, taking in her surroundings. What was it about that combination that turned a mere bathroom into a destination? Yet beyond the door awaited another, even grander destination, with a massive four-poster bed hung with curtains of lace and fine silks. She couldn't wait to bury herself deep under the comforter. She hadn't wanted to be here, but now that she was, there was no way she wasn't going to enjoy this unfamiliar taste of luxury.

Her stomach rumbled and she gave silent thanks for the healthy sign. Whatever illness or nerves had plagued her earlier today, at least now she could contemplate the notion of food without feeling like she wanted to throw up.

There was a faint knock from outside and Sienna opened the bathroom door a crack to hear a woman's voice advising in rusty English that her meal was ready. 'Thank you,' she called, 'I'll be right out.'

She towel-dried her hair until it settled into shaggy ringlets around her face and then rinsed out her underwear in the sink, hanging them over the towel rail. In this warm climate they would dry in no time.

Finally she unwrapped herself from the bath sheet and slipped on the silk robe she'd found hanging behind the door. She'd loved it from the moment she'd seen it hanging there, the jade green silk shot with gold thread, the vibrant shade changing subtly as the fabric moved under the light.

It felt every bit as good as it looked, the material gliding over her shoulders like a silken kiss, teasing her nipples into awareness with every soft shift of the fabric, reminding her all too well of Rafe and his magic touch...

Rafe.

He'd told her he wanted her again.

She sucked in a much needed burst of air. In the panic of not being able to get off the island, in her anger at being manipulated, she had let those words and her body's reaction to those words slide away. But she hadn't lost them at all. Instead the words had filtered down to a place deep inside her and taken root, sprouting questions like weeds.

He didn't really want her. He couldn't, she reasoned, answering one of those questions herself. Rafe was used to taking what he wanted and she was merely convenient. Available. A man like him would have no hesitation in assuming that after the first night they'd shared, she'd be willing to fall into his bed in a heartbeat.

Ready to discard in yet another.

He was merely toying with her, continuing that cat-and-mouse game he played so well, the predator enjoying the hunt.

He'd kept her here, prevented her from leaving, merely to continue the chase, because he damn well knew the longer he did, the more likely it would be that she would once again fall into his bed.

Sienna pulled the robe tighter around her, giving the tie at her waist a savage tug. She would not think about Rafe. At least, not that way. That other night was over. It was history. Rafe was nothing to her now but a mere inconvenience, and tomorrow she would be rid of even that.

She'd begun separating her hair into sections, preparing to braid it while still damp to control its natural curl, when the scent of food, fragrant and beguiling found its way into the bathroom. Her stomach rumbled again and she paused. It had been hours since she'd had a decent meal. Her hair could wait ten minutes; it wasn't as if she had other plans for the evening.

So she abandoned the braid, working her fingers through her still damp curls with one hand as she pulled open the bathroom door with the other.

'You look good enough to eat.'

She stopped dead, a *frisson* of fear shimmying its way down her spine, a sudden rush of heat pooling in that naked place between her thighs. She abandoned her hair and clutched the robe tighter around her, crossing her arms over her chest for good measure. 'What are you doing here?'

Rafe smiled at her as he transported dishes from a trolley onto a small table set by a window overlooking cliff-top and sea. A table covered in a lace tablecloth, complete with a floral centrepiece, a candle already lit amongst the flowers even though the evening was still young outside.

A table set for two.

'The chef has prepared his signature dishes for tonight's meal. I told him I would let him know personally what you thought.'

'I said, what are you doing here?'

He looked up at her ingenuously. 'Having dinner with you.'

'Even after I told you that I wouldn't dine with you.'

'No.' This time he stopped what he was doing and stood up straight, his eyes raking over her in such a way that she wondered if he could see right through the fabric to the truth of her state of undress beneath. 'What you actually said was that you would not join me for a meal. So I decided to join you instead.'

Anger welled up inside her, any hint of the relaxation afforded by the bath diminishing by the second. 'I made it plain that I had no wish to see you again tonight.'

He shrugged, that Mediterranean shrug that told her he cared not a damn for whatever she thought. 'I did not believe that was what you meant. You should know by now that you have a very expressive body. It told me otherwise.'

Heat flooded her face and she turned away, half regretting it when the sudden play of silk over skin sent her senses shimmering further into overdrive.

'You have no right—'

'I have every right! This is my principality, my island, my kingdom. Everything and everyone on it is subject to me. And that, my dear Sienna, whether you like it or not, includes you!'

She wheeled back around, grateful for his outburst. Anger was the reaction she'd wanted. Anger she could deal with. 'So now you fancy yourself as some petty despot and you've come to take what you think is yours. Well, sorry, but you don't suck me in with all that lord of the manor garbage.

Don't expect me to fall at your feet like some loyal subject grateful to have been asked to service her lord and master.'

His eyes glittered dangerously, a muscle in his jaw popped, and for a moment she feared she'd overstepped the mark. If he wanted to take her now, by force, who would come to her rescue? She was utterly alone here, in a world that was not her own, where the laws were not the laws she understood and where he was the master, the ruler of all.

But he'd never been a prince to her, just a man, and since his oh-so-rapid excision of her from his life, not a man she respected, let alone particularly cared for. So there was no way she would stoop to playing the game by his rules.

'Oh, I never assumed it would be that simple.'

His intentions thudded into her sensibilities with all the subtlety of cannon fire. Slowly she shook her head. 'I won't sleep with you,' she said, her voice abandoning her, leaving her with nothing more than a hoarse whisper.

'That remains to be seen.'

'I mean it, Rafe. Been there. Done that.'

'If you say so. So why don't we just concentrate on what we do agree on? Are you hungry, Sienna?'

Was he talking about food? The way he looked at her, his gaze warm on her skin, his eyes electric in their dark intensity, told her otherwise.

Her stomach chose that precise moment to make itself heard. Sienna shifted her arms over her stomach, but nothing could muffle the rumble, loud and insistent.

He smiled. 'Clearly you also have a beast that requires feeding. Come. Sit.'

She was hungry, so hungry that not even Rafe's presence could make a dint in it. But there was no way she was going to be comfortable enough to eat while clad only in a thin silk robe. No way in the world.

'I… I'll just get dressed.' She turned to collect her uniform where she'd left it lying on the bed, thinking that even without the underwear still drying in her bathroom, it would put more of a barrier between them than a mere whisper of silk.

But there was no uniform. She looked around, confused, sure she'd left it on the bed before her bath. She pulled open a closet door, thinking it might have been hung up, to find the closet devoid of everything but hangers.

'Is there a problem?' he asked behind her.

'My uniform. It's gone.'

'Why should you need it?'

'I left it on the bed, and now it's gone.'

'You seem to have an unusual knack for losing things. First, your helicopter. Now your uniform.'

She wheeled around, not fooled for a moment. 'You might consider this is all some sort of game, but I don't.'

'I assure you, this is no game.' His expression sent shock waves through her system, his voice set so low and deep that the words vibrated through her, and his eyes lit with an intensity that left her breathless. 'And just for the record,' he continued, letting his lips turn up into the barest of smiles, 'your uniform is in safe hands. It has merely been taken away for laundering. You will have it back by morning. Do you have a problem with clean clothes?'

Damn the man! 'Only that you expect me to sit down and dine wearing nothing more than a silk robe. Of course there's a problem!'

His eyes flared as they cruised hungrily over her robe like a heat-seeking missile. '*Nothing* more?'

She turned away, cursing herself for her inadvertent admission, but he didn't wait for her response. 'If you feel at a disadvantage, I could similarly divest myself of a few extraneous garments.' She turned back to see him make a move to start unbuttoning his shirt and she tossed her head, determined not to let him see just how much he'd rattled her. 'Don't be ridiculous! I didn't want, and wasn't expecting, company. What I meant is I'm hardly dressed for dinner.'

'On the contrary,' his eyes raking over her with all the subtlety of a hungry jungle cat, devouring her in a single heated glance, 'you are delightfully attired. Did anyone ever tell you how much those tones complement your colouring? You have the most beautiful skin,' he said, drawing close enough to touch the back of one finger to her cheek. 'Like the finest porcelain. So pale, almost translucent.'

Her heart was beating so loud she was sure he must hear it, her nipples so rock-like under their silken covering, there was no way he couldn't see them if he lowered his eyes.

But his gaze remained fixed on her face, searching her eyes, before lingering so long on her lips that they tingled under his scrutiny, so long that she realised she'd been holding her breath the entire time. Her lips parted as she drew in air, and suddenly his scent filled her and she could taste the man on her tongue, and the hunger she had been feeling changed direction.

He could kiss her now. The thought came from somewhere from the deep, dark recesses of her mind, somewhere forbidden and unwelcome. But the path was clear. He would kiss her, and she would accept his kiss, and then she would push her hands against his chest and be the one to break it off, before things went too far, before he assumed more than he already had.

But first—*oh, God yes*—first she would have that kiss.

The air crackled around her, heavy with expectation, every breath an eternity as his lips hovered so close to hers, the tug of his fingers through her hair and the glide of his nails against her scalp an exquisite torture.

And, as she gazed up at him, something skated across his

eyes, something that told her he thought he had her right where he wanted her, something that tugged her ability to reason right back from whatever dark place she'd temporarily locked it away.

And reason told her she'd been kidding herself. Because if she kissed him now, she'd never stop. If she put her hands up to his chest it wouldn't be to push him away, but to drink in the feel of his skin over muscled chest with her fingers. And one kiss would never be enough.

'You're right.' She mouthed the words, hardly recognising her own voice as she saw the answering question in his eyes, momentarily thrown off track.

'About what?'

It was her turn to smile. 'I'm famished.' She turned her head away, forced herself to move, clumsily at first, awkward in making her body move away from where it most wanted to be, before sinking gratefully into a chair. 'What's for dinner?'

Rafe watched her go, bemused by her sudden change of mood. Seconds ago she'd been his for the taking. Seconds ago the meal had been all but forgotten and promised to be long cold before they returned to it.

She wanted him, she'd made that more than plain with her parted lips and hitched breathing. She had wanted him then and she still wanted him, if the flame-red cheeks and the way she studiously refused to meet his eyes were any indication. She was just determined not to give in to it. Just like the last time, when she'd played hard to get.

But just like last time she would capitulate. And just like last time it would be worth the wait.

It wouldn't take long. He'd give her until the end of tonight's meal. And then he'd soon change her mind about leaving any time soon. One night had not been enough; he couldn't imagine it being enough again. And, after the last few frenetic weeks, he deserved a little relaxation. What better way to get it?

Rafe sighed as he joined her at the table, pulling a chilled bottle from the antique silver ice bucket before reaching over to pour her a glass of the local wine, already looking forward to the next few nights. He needed a distraction from worries about casinos and international financing and rebuilding the world's trust in Montvelatte. He needed something to persuade Sebastiano to ease off on the wife hunt. Just for a while.

'No,' she said, holding up one hand. 'No wine, please.'

He held up the bottle so that she could see the label. 'Are you sure? It's a vintage San Margarita Superiore, the island's pride and joy.'

She was shaking her head, the internationally acclaimed wine label with its clutch of gold-medal stickers from a dozen different wine shows clearly making no impression.

He moved the bottle and poured some of the straw-coloured liquid into his own glass. 'Are you worried I might get you drunk and try to seduce you?'

For the first time since he'd sat down, her eyes flicked up to meet his. 'Not at all. I'm worried I have to fly a helicopter tomorrow morning and I'm being professional. But if my caution stops me from doing something unwise into the deal, so much the better.'

He raised his eyebrows at her words, and at the opening she'd given him. 'And would this thing you might otherwise do be so unwise?'

She flicked a napkin in her fingers, unfolding it before letting it settle on her lap. 'I think so.'

'Even though it might also be very pleasurable?'

Her chin set, she turned those deep honey-coloured eyes up to his once again, any intended coolness belied by the twin slashes of red adorning her cheeks, and he knew she was remembering, as was he, just how pleasurable that night had been.

'It would be a mistake,' she said, her tone defiant, 'and wherever possible, I try to avoid making the same mistake twice.'

The words grated on his senses, as did her ability to turn defensiveness into attack. He replaced the bottle in the ice bucket with a satisfying crunch, half tempted to tell her she wasn't going anywhere tomorrow or any time soon until he was good and finished with her.

But as he'd seen before, that would merely fuel her resistance. And he didn't want resistance. He wanted her warm and willing and begging him to fill her. And he wanted it all tonight.

Rafe forced a smile to his lips as he raised his glass to her in a toast. 'Then we must ensure you are not tempted to repeat any of the so-called mistakes of the past. Please, eat up.'

Sienna did eat up, as course after course of the most amazing food was delivered steaming-hot to her door. And she knew it must be amazing from the descriptions he gave her along the way, though she never tasted a thing, not the crayfish-filled ravioli or the lightly dusted tender calamari. Even the most succulent quail was completely wasted on her. The fine textures she could appreciate, but nothing of the taste.

Not with him sitting there, so close, so larger than life.

A man she had slept with once before.

A man who had made it plain that he wanted to sleep with her again.

And, if she were true to herself, a man who, despite everything, tempted her more than she cared to admit.

'Why did Signorina Genevieve come today?' she asked, as she contemplated the stunning dessert that had been placed before her. Fresh berries and cream lay sandwiched between wafers of meringue, creating a tower of colour and summer delights circled with a raspberry coulis and sprinkled with icing sugar, and she honestly wished she could appreciate it more, but the question had been circling through Sienna's thoughts for some time. That and the reason for the woman's sudden departure from the island so soon after arriving. The young woman had been in good spirits during their flight, and, even though she hadn't spoken a word to Sienna, it had been clear through her animated conversation with her mother how excited she had been to be travelling to Montvelatte. Sienna had figured her own reason for the visit, but given her sudden departure, now she wasn't so sure. 'Surely she would have stayed longer.'

Across the table Rafe leaned back, dragging in a breath. He crossed fingers in his lap, even though she could tell by the tightness of his shoulders that he wasn't as relaxed as he made out. 'She came for an interview, that's all.'

'She was applying for a job?'

This time he gave an ironic laugh. 'You could say that. My adviser seems to be obsessed with finding Montvelatte a princess. Which unfortunately involves finding me a wife.'

'A wife?' Sienna dragged in her own breath and fiddled with the placement of her napkin. *Rafe was getting married?*

She should have seen it coming. It wasn't a constant supply of high-class mistresses he'd had ferried to the island over the last couple of weeks—since when did they take their mothers with them?—it was potential brides.

And somehow that was no relief at all.

She did her best to inject some amusement into her voice. 'And this is how princes of Montvelatte find their wives, is it? By interview? How very romantic.'

Rafe reached for his wine glass and swirled the white wine in lazy circles, but he didn't take a sip. 'Romance doesn't enter the equation. A direct Lombardi descendant must take the throne, or the principality loses its right to exist. This is all about ensuring that doesn't happen.'

'That sounds very melodramatic.'

'Simply fact. Montvelatte's right to exist is predicated on the continuation of the line.'

'So that's where you came in.'

He leaned back in his chair. 'Even bastards have a purpose, it seems.'

His self-deprecating manner didn't fool her for a second. 'That's what was happening—that night—when the news broke on the television and they carted away your two half-brothers. You knew then, didn't you? You knew what it meant.'

'I had a gut feeling I might get a call.'

'And you just couldn't wait to take over the reins and put on that crown.'

He raised the glass to his lips and, without taking his eyes from hers, drank down the wine. 'You think I wanted this? To have my life turned into public property?'

'You seem happy enough lording it over me, holding me here against my will and forcing your way into my room when you're not welcome. Seems to me you're a natural at playing to the manor born.'

He stared at her a while, his eyelids half closed. 'If you say so.'

'And now you must have a wife. To give you an heir and to give Montvelatte the breathing space it needs.'

'That's right.'

She toyed with her dessert, making lazy figure eights through the raspberry coulis that lapped at the edges of her triumph in chocolate. 'So you're "interviewing" prospective wives. And meanwhile you're dining with a woman you once spent a night with, and who you have every intention of sleeping with again.'

It was meant to be an accusation, something that put him at a disadvantage, but the way he looked at her, the sudden widening and wanting revealed in his eyes, the planes of his face suddenly harsher in the fading light, more dangerous seemed to have the opposite effect. 'I am.'

And she felt a rush of heat infuse her skin, throbbing in places that responded eagerly to his words like an invitation. She was a fool for walking into his trap, for bringing up the one thing he'd somehow avoided talking about all night, and yet the one thing she knew he expected to happen. She looked down at her plate helplessly, at the dessert she'd barely touched, and knew there was no escape there. There were no more courses to come, the coffee already poured, the *petit fours* sitting between them accusingly. Dinner had come to an end and now he would expect her to fall into bed with him.

He needed a wife. He wanted a bed warmer. And it was clear whatever place she occupied fell into the latter category.

By rights she should hate him for it.

She *did* hate him for it.

And yet...

His gaze washed over her in a heated rush. He didn't have to utter another word; the question was there in his eyes, the hunger, the need. The promise of bliss.

Memories of the night they'd spent together surged back, rushing over her like a king tide, deep and unable to be resisted, a force of nature that could not be denied. What he'd done to her with his hands and his mouth and his perfect body. The way he'd made her feel...

The knowledge of how he could make her feel again.

Was it so wrong to feel so tempted? Was it so wrong for her body to hunger for more of what he'd given her, to experience more of that particular brand of magic?

She was leaving tomorrow.

She could have one more night. Where was the harm in that? One more night, and this time she would do the leaving. There could be no more surprises, no more disappointments. This time he wouldn't have the chance to dump her. This time she would be the one to walk away, the one in control. She could leave him to his ladies and his princesses and contessas. One of them would ultimately win him for ever, but she could have him right here, right now.

Maybe it would never be enough. But wouldn't one more night be at least something for the inconvenience he'd put her through today?

She deserved something. Surely.

He chose that exact moment to extend his hand to her. 'It's time.'

CHAPTER FIVE

'COME,' Rafe said, his voice rumbling through her in a series of tremors that threatened to unravel what was left of her defences. His long fingers wrapped around hers, circling her hand, drawing her up from her chair and against the black-clad, lethal length of him.

'Rafe,' she said, as his body received her in a swaying motion, almost as if dancing to a slow, silent waltz. 'Shh,' he whispered. 'Don't say anything.'

She couldn't say anything anyway, her reason for speaking forgotten while her senses were fully employed drinking in the feel of him moving against her, setting the silk robe to a sensual massage against her tight nipples and aching breasts.

Intoxicating.

His touch was like a drug, she decided, his hands dispensing a sensual dose everywhere they glided, everywhere they touched. And when he kissed her it was with the promise of ecstasy.

Sienna melted against him, his mouth taking possession of hers, hot and wanting and so hungry that she wanted to give him everything she had, if only he would give her more of him.

His fingers splayed wide down the curve of her spine and over her behind, holding her to him and against that rock-hard evidence of his need. She invited herself still closer, as his lips left her mouth to trail kisses down her throat. Her head fell back and he took advantage, sliding the silk of her robe apart, grazing the flesh above her breast with his teeth.

It was everything she'd dreamed of. Everything she'd missed in these last few weeks.

Make the most of it, a tiny voice in her head told her. *Because it's all you're ever going to get.*

A hand cupped her breast and she gasped, the voice in her head vanquished. 'You're more beautiful than I remembered,' Rafe murmured huskily, rolling one aching nipple between his thumb and finger before dipping his head to capture it between his lips.

Pleasure, exquisite and intense, speared deep inside, setting off a bloom of moisture between her thighs. She clung to him, knowing that otherwise her knees would give out and she would fall.

He turned his attention to her other breast, sweeping the fabric from her skin, letting her robe fall open in the process, uncaring, his hands underneath, across her naked skin. He drew back then and drank her in with his eyes, and the raw intensity she saw there terrified her.

She shivered, the tiny voice once again uppermost in her mind. What kind of man was he that he could look at her like that and then calmly turn around and marry another?

What kind of woman was she to let him?

She'd told him she wouldn't sleep with him. And yet here she was, next to naked, all but begging for him to take her. She was akin to a starving dog under the table, grateful for any scraps that might be thrown her way.

What the hell was wrong with her?

Sienna wrenched her hands from his shoulders, trusting her spine was firmer now and that her legs would hold up on their own, and pulled the sides of her robe together, lashing her arms firmly below her breasts to keep it there. She was shaking and she couldn't stop it, her body protesting at the sudden change of direction.

His head tilted to one side, his brows drawing together in a frown. 'Sienna,' he said straightening, 'are you cold?'

She shook her head, shuffling her bare feet backwards over the rich Persian carpet. 'I think you should go. This is a really bad idea.'

His eyes glinted menacingly. 'You didn't seem to think so a moment ago.'

'I told you before I wouldn't sleep with you. I'm sorry, but I haven't changed my mind.'

He took a step closer, the knot in his brows deepening. 'What kind of game are you playing? It's obvious you want this as much as I do.'

'No. I don't think so. And personally I don't think you give a damn what I want. All you care about is an easy lay.'

He growled at her coarse words. 'That's not true.'

'It is true! You decided when I landed on this island that you had an easy lay on tap. You didn't give a damn what I thought then, and you don't give a damn now. I told you I wanted off this island then and I still want off this island now. But you're still not listening. You still think you can take whatever you damn well please. Well, let me tell you, you had your chance in Paris and you made your choice crystal clear then.'

He didn't move, other than the faint tic in his jaw and the dangerous gleam in his eyes. 'Don't think you're going to gain some advantage by holding out. I'm afraid Sebastiano's short-list of potential Montvelatte princesses is already complete. There's a place for you in my bed if you want to take it, but I certainly won't beg you to change your mind.'

Cold fury at his arrogance skyrocketed her anger into overdrive. 'You think I want to marry you? Get real! I don't care that you're a prince. I wouldn't care if you were the Beast of Iseo himself. I wouldn't marry you if you were the last man left on earth. I told you I wouldn't sleep with you and I won't. Get used to it!'

His face was dark and filled with a fury that secretly terrified her. He was a prince. This was his land, his world and she was telling him how it was to be. She must be insane to think she could get away with it. But damn it, nothing gave him the excuse to act the way he did.

Nothing!

He glowered at her again, took a step closer that had her wanting to reel right away, before his tightly drawn lips finally gave way to sound. 'Have it your way.'

It was a perfect day, the rising sun already high in the sky, dazzling with the promise of heat. The infinity pool set into the gardens below sparkled and merged with the sea beyond, the perfect diamante-set blue, which in turn merged into a perfect azure sky.

A perfect day. And the perfectly wrong day for a foul mood.

Rafe sat on the terrace, holding his coffee, staring out resentfully over the beauty of the surroundings. His plans to seduce her into submission had come unstuck. So be it. If she wanted out so badly, she could have it. It was no real loss.

The chopper waited on the helipad for its pilot. He'd watched its arrival half an hour ago. He was surprised, given her vehemence of last night, that she hadn't already left.

He took a sip. *Dio!* Even the coffee tasted bitter today. He put down his cup with a clatter and stood. What was he waiting for? She was leaving. He wouldn't give her the satisfaction of seeing him watching out for her departure.

Something made him turn then, a noise, a movement, and

he saw her, standing in the doorway staring at him like a frightened animal stuck in the glare of oncoming headlights. Memories of last night's argument bubbled up like boiling mud, and his gut squeezed tight.

The only compensation was that she looked as bad as he felt. Her skin was pale. So pale against the Titian gold framing her face, even though pulled tight into that damned braid she favoured. And her eyes were smudged with dark circles that spoke of a lack of sleep that he could only hope matched his own.

What was she so scared of? Did she think he'd make another move on her? Not a chance!

'I just wanted to say goodbye,' she said, in a voice so tiny it almost got lost in the space between them.

He gave a brief nod. 'Have you eaten?'

Her face seemed to lose even more colour, if that were possible, and as he looked closer, he could see she was clutching at the door beside her for support, her grip so tight that her knuckles were white.

She shook her head, her lips pressed tightly together, her whole face looking pinched and drawn. She'd had a worst night than he had. *Good.* But as he edged nearer, he noticed for the first time that there was colour in her face after all, a strange shade of grey. 'Shouldn't you have breakfast before you go? At least some coffee?'

'I have to go,' she squeezed out between barely open lips, her eyes wider than ever as he approached. 'Thank you for your… Well, thank you.'

He nodded again, determined not to care one way or another how she felt. 'I'll have Sebastiano take you down to the helipad.'

She nodded and turned to go then, letting go of the side of the door to melt back into the house, but something about the way she moved, a slight stagger, a waver in her step, had him at her side in a heartbeat.

He reached for her arm, felt the momentary resistance in her slight frame before she sagged against him in a dead faint.

'Sebastiano,' he yelled, collecting her into his arms. 'Get the doctor!'

'She's resting now.'

Rafe stopped pretending not to be interested at the sound of the *dottore's* voice.

'Is she all right?'

'She's fine, but I've advised her to get a complete check-up when she gets home. And to think about avoiding flying while she feels like this, of course. But she'll feel better a little later on in the day. That's usually how morning sickness works.'

Clouds of black filled the space behind Rafe's eyes, an unexpected explosion of red following close behind as his heart pumped loud in his chest. 'She's pregnant, then?'

'Six to eight weeks, at a guess,' replied the doctor, oblivious to the bombshell he'd just dropped. 'So if you can do anything to reduce her stress levels, that will probably help her through this period. She does present as being very stressed.'

The doctor continued his diagnosis but Rafe heard nothing. Not while his mind processed the news, peeling back time, trying to remember. *Six to eight weeks.* Was it possible?

He'd used protection. He would never be that careless.

Except he hadn't!

He had been that careless.

The details came back in a blinding flash. He'd heard of his half-brothers' arrests and of their implication in their father's death. He'd learned that Montvelatte's existence balanced on a knife edge. And he'd been blind with anger and fury and rage that they could have been so arrogant and so self-absorbed that they had done this with pure greed in mind, and that they hadn't seen where they were heading. So blind with anger that he hadn't stopped to think, hadn't hesitated before burying himself one last time deep inside the woman who'd just happened to be there.

Had that momentary loss of control done this, resulted in a child? Was it his?

She'd almost got away. He'd been that close to letting her go, angry that she could deny him the pleasure he'd find with her, and so close to letting her walk out of his life for ever.

Would he ever have found out if she'd gone? She might never have told him.

Six weeks. Coincidence? Or fate?

Whichever, she wasn't getting away before he found out for sure.

The doctor had finished his report. 'Can I see her?'

'Certainly. Though be gentle. Right now she's a little emotionally fragile.'

Rafe blew out his breath in a rush. 'I'll just bet she is.'

Moments later he paused outside her room, his anger festering inside him, a living thing. He'd paced the terrace for endless minutes, working out the possibilities. If she'd told him last night that she was pregnant with someone else's child, if she'd thrown it in his face then and there, he would have left her alone. But she hadn't said a word. And six to eight weeks? Surely she must have known something? Was that the real reason she'd declined to have any wine?

He thought back on her determination to escape the island. She'd been desperate to get away. So desperate to escape that she'd risk flying a helicopter when she was in danger of passing out at the controls. If those facts weren't enough to spell out her guilt, he didn't know what was.

She didn't want him to know.

Which could only mean one thing.

It had to be his.

He hauled in a lungful of air, felt the oxygen fuel the fury inside him until it was in danger of combusting, until he wanted to howl at the irony.

All that time Sebastiano had been doing his utmost to find Montvelatte the perfect breeding stock.

All that time Sebastiano had spent ensuring Montvelatte would not be left without an heir.

And all that time there had been one all along.

It was a disaster. Sienna pushed herself back into pillows damp with tears, unable to assimilate the new-found knowledge, unable to come to terms with the physician's declaration.

There was nothing wrong with her, he'd calmly informed her, in the very same breath he'd dropped the bombshell that she was pregnant and suffering nothing more debilitating than morning sickness.

Nothing wrong. That was a laugh, when her entire world was shattering to pieces around her. Nothing wrong, when, in fact, nothing could be less right.

And so she'd argued and remonstrated with him. It had been too late in her cycle and she'd had a period, admittedly light, but then she'd only just come off the pill. It couldn't be possible.

And the doctor had looked benignly down at her as he'd clicked up his bag and explained that there was no mistake, that coming off the pill so recently meant her cycle could be late, and that the light period she'd assumed she'd had was most likely no more than an implantation bleed.

And then he'd asked her what she did for a living and warned her that she might have to think about not flying for a while. *Not flying?* Flying was her job. She'd just got the job of her dreams. It was her life!

And now she knew that the churning in her stomach was nothing to do with any morning sickness, but a gut-wrenching reaction to the news.

She was pregnant. With Rafe's child. That alone was bad enough. But he wasn't just a man any more.

He was a prince.

She screwed her face into the pillow and tried unsuccessfully to stem a fresh batch of tears. This couldn't be happening to her. Not with him. Not now.

He might be the father of the baby growing inside her, but he was expected to marry. Someone suitable. Someone worthy of being Montvelatte's princess.

Someone else.

Not some no-name commoner from a dysfunctional family who'd spent one night with him and ended up pregnant.

Which was fine, because she didn't damn well want any man on those terms anyway.

Sienna sniffed and sat up, grabbing a tissue to wipe away the moisture on her cheeks and blow her nose. Damn it all. Lying here crying wouldn't help; she had to pull herself together and get moving. She shoved back the covers and eased herself up to sitting on the side of the bed, swallowing air, waiting until the rocking motion inside her settled before she trusted her feet to hold her up.

Rafe wanted her gone from the island, he'd made that crystal clear, so she would oblige. And, let's face it, the last thing either he or Montvelatte needed right now was the scandal of an unplanned pregnancy with someone unsuitable. So she would get dressed and fly back to Genoa as soon as this damned nausea settled down. As soon as she'd come to terms with the shock of this latest bombshell.

Except that she was pregnant.

How was anyone supposed to terms with something like that?

There was a sharp rap on the door before it swung open, revealing the person she least wanted to see in the world. Her heart slammed into his chest as his dark eyes honed in on her, intent but frustratingly unreadable. *Please God, the doctor had not shared her news!*

She was dressed in some kind of white nightgown that fitted over her breasts and then fell softly to her ankles and he gave a silent tick of approval for whoever had released her hair from that damned braid so now it rioted around her face in a mass of colour and curl.

She looked like a virgin on her way to a sacrifice.

And then he took in her wide red-rimmed eyes, the eyes that looked up at him with something akin to terror, and revised the description. She looked like hell. *As guilty as hell.*

'What are you doing out of bed?'

'I was just getting up,' she protested, through lips inordinately pale. 'Or I was, until you once again decided to invite yourself in unannounced. So if you'll excuse me, I'd like to get dressed.'

'I thought you were sick.'

'I'm feeling much better,' she replied, adding a smile that didn't go near to erasing the caginess in those hazel eyes. 'I'm sorry. I don't know what came over me back there. I…I must have eaten something that disagreed with me.'

He almost growled. She was still trying to hide the truth. 'So now you're accusing my cook of poisoning you?'

'No! I didn't mean—' She gave up trying and shook her head. 'Look, I'm sorry to put you out, but I'll be gone soon. So if you wouldn't mind…'

She gestured towards the door but he wasn't going anywhere. He stood at the foot of the bed and leant a hand against one of the carved wooden posts. 'I don't think so. I really think leaving would be unwise right now.'

Sienna stood up in a rush and sprang away from the bed, a blur of motion as the white gown billowed around her long legs like a cloud, her bare feet pacing the carpet. He could almost see her mind ticking over as her hands busied themselves collecting her hair into a loose pony tail before letting it go to spring back wild around her face again. 'Look, Rafe,' she said, turning to him, the colour of irritation high on cheeks that otherwise looked too pale to be human, 'we've been through all this and I'm fed up with the way you think you can push me around. You agreed last night that I could leave today and, quite frankly, it won't be soon enough. As soon as I'm dressed, I'm out of here.' She was halfway to the bathroom before he caught up with her, catching her arm and swinging her around.

'Not with my baby, you're not.'

He heard her gasp. Smelt her fear. 'What are you talking about?' She was still fighting, but the guilt was there, in the defensive sheen in her eyes, in the faint tremor in her lips.

'Why didn't you tell me you were pregnant?'

Her breathing was shallow and fast, her chest rising and falling rapidly with the action. 'I don't know why you think it's any of your business, but maybe I didn't know.'

'You're lying.'

'Then maybe it's not your baby? Did you ever stop to consider that?'

He reeled back as if she'd physically lashed out, but only for a moment, before the feral gleam in his eye returned. 'You went from my bed to another's? I don't believe you.'

'You threw me out. Why should you care who I sleep with?'

'I care because I do not believe you. You were hiding it from me and you're still trying to. It's my baby, isn't it? You're having my baby!'

If he hadn't sensed her need, if he hadn't let her go, she

would never have made it to the bathroom in time. There was precious little in her stomach, nothing more than dry toast and some of the same sweet tea she'd had yesterday that had been so soothing at the time. And yet it felt like she was being torn apart from the inside with each violent heave.

And he was there, holding back her hair and steadying her shoulders as she held onto the bowl for grim death.

Oh, God, if it wasn't bad enough that Rafe should see her like this, the doctor had obviously told him why.

A total disaster had just got worse.

At last it was over; the thrashing of her stomach calmed. She heard the sound of running water, felt the cool press of a flannel against her face and she took it gratefully, pressing it to her tear-stained cheeks and wishing that there was something that could so easily soothe her soul.

The doctor had told him, and Rafe knew!

What the hell was she supposed to do now?

'Let's get you back to bed,' he said, helping her to rise on unsteady legs and steering her from the room. She went with him, the fight gone from her, her strength drained, her mind numb with it.

'I'm sorry,' she said, as he eased her down on the bed, knowing that a terrible wrong had been done, knowing she was at least partly responsible, not having a clue what to say. Having even less idea of how to fix it. 'I realize this is inconvenient. I'll go. I won't tell anyone, I promise.'

And the band that had bound his gut ever since he had heard she was pregnant grew even tighter, until even his lungs felt squeezed with the pressure. Better than any test result, it was the final confirmation he needed, banishing any lingering doubts in an instant. 'So it is mine!'

Her eyes looked up at him, pained and dull. 'Nobody will ever know. I promise.'

'*Merda!* I will know! Or are you already planning on disposing of the "inconvenience", as you so clinically put it, in order to assure that outcome?'

Her eyes sparked with indignation, their hazel lights suddenly flashing gold as if someone had thrown a switch, though her skin was still deathly pale and her voice was still rough and raw. 'As it happens I haven't had a chance to consider my options, but just what kind of person do you think I am?'

'It doesn't matter what type of person I think you are. What matters is what you plan on doing with my child.'

'And I'm supposed to believe you care? Don't bother. I promise not to go to the papers or get in the way of your precious princess hunt.'

'No.'

'What do you mean, "no"?'

'It means that's not good enough. I will not allow another generation of Lombardi bastard children to be cast aside as if they are not family. There is only one solution.'

She rolled her head from side to side against the pillow. 'You can share access, if that's what you want. I can hardly deny a child access to its father.'

'I'm glad you understand that. And there is no better way to share access…' he smiled, amazed at how neatly the whole thing fitted together—a woman he had no trouble desiring, already pregnant with his child, and an end to Sebastiano's endless round of prospective wife interviews, all rolled into one neat solution '…than to make you my wife.'

CHAPTER SIX

IF SIENNA hadn't been lying down, her knees would have given way beneath her. As it was, the breath was punched from her lungs. He couldn't be serious!

'You have to be joking. There's no reason on earth why I should marry you.'

'It is the only solution. I need a wife and an heir.'

'You need a princess, not a pilot. You need someone off that list of titled wannabes.'

'But you have something they can only promise. You have conveniently proven your ability to conceive.'

'Forget it. There's no way I'm marrying you just because I'm pregnant. No way in the world.'

'You need not be frightened of the royalty angle. You will be coached in our language and history.'

'I wouldn't say yes even if you weren't a prince! A baby is no basis for a marriage. I would never do that to a child.'

'And yet you would be happy to let that child grow up without its father. How is that fairer?'

'You can't force me to do this. Your father never married your mother simply because she was pregnant.'

'He didn't think he needed to. He already had his heir and a spare. My sister and I were surplus to requirements.'

'But your mother—'

'Had no choice! She received a substantial settlement and an annual pension on the condition she never returned to Montvelatte, and she never told anyone who her children's father was.'

Sienna threw back her chin. 'I would be more than happy to comply with the same conditions. For nothing. It wouldn't cost you a thing.'

He shook his head. 'You are kidding yourself. There is no way I would allow you to bring up our child in near poverty.'

'I have a job!'

'For how long? How can you fly in the condition you found yourself this morning? How long do you think anyone will employ a pilot who could faint at any minute? Who in their right mind would want to fly with you?'

'I have some savings. I'll take time off. Morning sickness doesn't last forever.'

'And after the baby comes, how do you expect to keep working when you have a child to care for?'

'Like plenty of other woman in my situation do. I'll cope.'

'Not with my child. Simply coping is not an option. How long do you think you'll keep the origins of your baby secret?'

'Your mother obviously managed to.'

'More than thirty years ago when there was still a measure of respect for privacy. Whereas these days, any hint of scandal, any hint of a royal baby born out of wedlock and the paparazzi will come baying at your door. How long do you think you can hide the truth?'

'I won't tell anyone if you won't!'

'And when I marry and have a wife and a family, and then the truth inevitably comes out because of something the doctor today tells his secretary or his wife, you would be happy to humiliate the woman I married with the news that I already had a child? How do you think that would look splashed across the gutter press? How do you think this child will feel when he learns that he was the rightful heir of Montvelatte and you denied him that birthright?'

'Why do you assume it will be a boy?'

'It doesn't matter. Girl or boy, you will be denying this child its place in the Montvelattian monarchy.'

'Only if it finds out. And who is going to tell?'

His arms came down on the bed either side of her, his face bare inches from her own, and it was all she could do not to cower back into the pillows at the anger and pain so starkly reflected in his features.

'I will tell. Do not think you can deny me access to my child simply because you would rather forget who his father is. I am not like my father. I will not abandon a child I sired or hide it away merely because I was not married to its mother.'

Sienna watched his eyes while he made his speech, watched the way the pain coursed so deeply through them. He'd missed out on having a father all his life. He'd been cast away, exiled with his mother, unwanted by the father who'd sired him.

And he was right. One way or another, no matter how close she played her cards to her chest, there was no way she could shut Rafe out of her child's life. But in allowing Rafe access to her child, there was no way its parentage could ever be kept secret.

So where did that leave her?

It was all too much to take in. She'd only just discovered she was pregnant, and now he was demanding that she marry him, a man she'd spent one short night with and the last twenty-four hours trying to get away from, a man who would, without a second thought, bully her into a marriage she neither wanted nor needed.

A shotgun wedding, just like her mother's. Except this

time there were no parents holding a gun to Rafe's head to persuade him to do the right thing by their daughter. This time it was Rafe holding a gun to her head.

Was it because it was the right thing to do by their child? Or was it simply because it was convenient to him?

Either way, his wanting to marry her clearly had nothing to do with her.

'You can't make me do this.' She'd wanted to sound strong and sure but her voice came out sounding more like a plea.

'It's the only thing to do. I'll inform Sebastiano and have him make the necessary arrangements.'

The necessary arrangements? Rafe had it sounding like a royal wedding was no more hassle than a trip to the local corner store.

'No! I haven't agreed to anything. You can't make me do this.'

'You have no choice.'

'I have a choice! I'm leaving and you can't stop me.' She scooted to the other side of the bed, swinging her legs over the side and pushing herself off, but he was already there, standing in front of here like a storm cloud, angry and potent and thunderous. But the hand he put to her face was gentle and warm, and she trembled into his touch. His eyes studied her face, his thumb traced the line of her lips, and her heartbeat jagged, and when his words came, it was more a promise than a threat.

'Leave and I will bring you back. Run and I will catch you. There is no escaping the truth of this, Sienna. You will marry me. You will become my wife.'

She looked up at him, afraid to blink, afraid to breathe, lest she broke this spell he'd somehow woven around her. How long he stood there stroking her face, how long she allowed him to, she didn't know. And only the sense that she was losing herself, spinning out of control into a place with no horizons, into a place she had no way of navigating her way out of, shot a burst of fear straight to her heart.

'There has to be another way,' she whispered.

His hand cupping her jaw, he dipped his face to hers and pressed the barest of kisses to her lips. 'There is no other way.'

Sebastiano wasn't so sure. He took the news of the cancellation of the remaining marriage candidates and the reason with the look of a man heading for the gallows. 'Are you sure this is wise, Prince Raphael, to marry such a woman? The role of Princess of Montvelatte is a demanding one. What background and training has this woman had in the skills necessary to undertake such a role?'

'I would imagine the same amount of training that I received in becoming Montvelatte's Prince. And yet nobody questioned my qualifications.'

'You have royal blood, Highness. There is a difference.'

'And she carries it!'

His aide gave a brief cough into his hand, too pointed to miss. 'You have something to say, Sebastiano?'

'Merely that I think it would be wise to guarantee that fact before we make any announcements.'

Rafe had no doubt. The way she'd reacted to his accusations, the way she'd apologized and promised to keep it quiet—he had no doubt at all. But Sebastiano needed facts, and it was better that they did the digging before some gossip magazine got there before them. 'Arrange for whatever tests you need—even a date will help to confirm the truth—and meanwhile find out all you can about her—her past, her boyfriends, and anyone she's seen apart from me in the last eight weeks.'

Sebastiano nodded, looking more satisfied than he had all day, and gave a little bow. 'It will be done.'

Rafe watched him take his leave and felt a pang of regret that one had to be so careful, knowing it had to be done, and knowing equally that if there was any dirt to be had on Sienna Wainwright, Sebastiano would dig it out.

He just hoped there was none.

Sienna picked up the telephone in the library and listened for a dial tone, hoping that, unlike the phone in her room, this one would not be switched through to the housekeeper. Satisfied, she nervously dialled the direct number of her boss at Sapphire Blue Charters and waited what felt like agonizing seconds for the call to be answered.

She'd been thinking about it all night. She had no way of getting to the town except by foot and she had no doubt that Rafe would find her and bring her back as promised, even if she'd had the money to buy a fare off the island. And there was no point calling the police, because the palace guard were the ones who'd threatened to arrest her if she didn't accompany them to the Castello in the first place. Asking for help from the Australian Embassy was tantamount to taking out a full page ad, and that was hardly the way she wanted to slip quietly out of Rafe's life. But Monsieur Rocher might send a helicopter, once he knew she was being held against her will.

'*Oui?*' The grunting voice of the owner-manager of Sapphire Blue greeted her.

She took a deep breath and crossed the fingers of her free hand. '*Monsieur Rocher, c'est moi, Sienna Wainwright. Je suis désolé—*'

'*Bonjour*, Sienna!'

Sienna listened in amazement as the tongue-lashing she was expecting turned into high praise as she learned she had been retained on an ongoing basis as Montvelatte's private pilot, and for three times the going rate, in response to which Monsieur Rocher had awarded her employee of the month.

'Mais non—'

But Monsieur Rocher was too full of praise to be interrupted. He wished her well, thanked her for her good work and bade her a hasty, *'Au revoir'*, before the line went dead.

'Can I help you with something?'

Sienna turned, still reeling from the phone call, to find Sebastiano standing in the doorway, his expression looking anything but helpful. Quickly she replaced the receiver, knowing she'd been caught out. 'I…I was just calling my boss.'

'So I gathered. And did you find everything to your satisfaction.'

'I've been made employee of the month.'

He gave a slight mocking bow. 'Congratulations.'

Sienna straightened. It was clear from just his tone that Sebastiano didn't welcome her presence here, but then little wonder if she'd put paid to his plans of Rafe marrying someone from the noble classes. She could take offence that he clearly thought her unbefitting of the role of Montvelatte's Princess, or she could use it for her own purposes.

She laced her fingers together and took a step closer. 'Sebastiano, maybe you *can* help me.'

His eyes honed in on her suspiciously. 'In what way?'

'You could help get me off the island.'

This time those eyes narrowed, and he looked around before closing the door behind him. 'To what purpose?'

'So Rafe can marry someone more suitable.' She saw the glimmer in his eyes that betrayed how appealing he found her words.

'But you are carrying Prince Raphael's child, are you not?'

'It's still me he would be marrying.'

His expression remained guarded, suspicious, while his

eyes looked thoughtful. Then he shook his head. 'I'm afraid I cannot help you. But if you would like to make any more phone calls, perhaps you should know that all calls to and from the Castello are monitored for security reasons.'

Sienna shivered. So that was how he'd found her. 'Thank you, Sebastiano. So if I call my landlady to enquire after my apartment?'

'Please, feel free. But you will discover that your rent has been paid and your personal belongings sent for, to make your stay here more comfortable.'

'Thank you,' she said, *I think,* allowing herself to be led away, and feeling the noose around her neck growing tighter by the minute.

The next day under the trellised vines shading the terrace, Sienna daydreamed, thinking back to a time she could only imagine, another time when her mother had discovered she was pregnant, with a marriage to Sienna's father hastily arranged in that discovery's wake.

Had her mother felt this terror, this fear of having a new life growing inside her and all the unknowns that went with it? Had she been secretly afraid of the prospect of marrying a man who had blown into town on the tide? Or had love blinded her to those fears, so that the prospect of marrying the man she had fallen head over heels in love with, and of bearing him a child, was so utterly exciting that she'd had no doubts?

She'd been so young, barely eighteen at the time and eight years younger than Sienna was now. Surely she must have had doubts, no matter how much she'd thought she'd loved him? Surely she must have wondered if the wanderlust father of her child could ever really change?

'It's time for your ultrasound.'

Rafe's voice intruded into her thoughts, and she blinked,

the present world suddenly coming back into sharp focus as she looked up and he filled her vision, instantly kicking new life into her heart rate. How he still had that effect on her when she was basically his prisoner here, she couldn't understand and didn't want to analyse. She only knew that the sooner she could put a lid on this inner turmoil she felt whenever he so much as looked at her, the better.

To him she might only be the vessel that carried his child, and a convenient solution to a problem that threatened the Principality, but there was no way she could consider marriage to a man like Rafe—a prince—in such clinical terms. And yet if she was going to have to go through with this, she needed to be able to.

A strange fear zipped up her spine. The fact she was even considering marrying Rafe—when had that change in her thinking taken place? And more importantly, why? It was anathema to her—marrying for the sake of a child—and yet she was entertaining the idea as if it were a done deal. Last night again she'd thought about getting help. Why shouldn't she call the Embassy, and who cared if the calls were monitored? By the time they discovered who she was calling, help could be on its way, and to hell with the fall out. He had no right to keep her here against her will.

And again she'd shut herself in the library, meaning to call, fully intending to. But she'd only got as far as lifting the receiver. Only pressed it to her ear, before the fingers of her other hand had cut the connection, and she'd slammed the receiver down in frustration.

What was happening to her?

Three days she'd been on the island now. Yesterday had been filled with an endless parade of specialists, nutritionists and exercise gurus, and she'd met Carmelina, the dark-haired young beauty who was to 'manage' her new wardrobe, and lay out whatever outfits she'd need in readiness for the day's and evening's activities. When she'd protested that she'd successfully managed her wardrobe by herself for the best part of twenty years, Rafe had reminded her that soon she would be a princess, dressing for all manner of events, formal and informal, and that she could not be expected to manage a wardrobe the size of a department store.

And when a fashion consultant arrived, bringing along an entire boutique and three assistants with her and fitted Sienna out in an entire wardrobe in under two hours—and that was only the beginning, she'd assured her, planning on returning with designs made solely for her—Sienna finally believed him.

Today promised to be more of the same. Was it any wonder she felt numb from all the attention? Once yesterday's obstetrician had confirmed her pregnancy, this juggernaut that was to be a royal wedding rolled and gained momentum with every minute.

And she was still only just coming to terms with her pregnancy. Once again this morning, she'd felt nauseous, though it was more a general queasiness this time that had assailed her, a queasiness that paled in comparison to the illness of those first days here. How much had stress and high emotions played a part in that—the fear of meeting Rafe again, her fury at being held against her will and the accusation that she'd kept her pregnancy secret from him—had this all combined to magnify the worst of her pregnancy symptoms tenfold?

'Sienna?' He put out a hand to her, obviously impatient to see the proof of the child they had conceived together. 'Come.'

She regarded it suspiciously. He hadn't made a move to touch her yesterday, not after he'd discovered she was pregnant and they'd shared that one brief kiss. Out of consideration for her condition? She wondered. It wouldn't surprise her if he figured he didn't need to touch her now, his work already done.

Nevertheless she slipped her fingers into his and let him lead her inside, amazed at how comfortable his grip felt, and how much warmth could be conveyed in the touch of just one hand. It was almost enough to make her forget the litre of water she'd been asked to drink and the knowledge of where that litre of fluid now resided. Almost.

'Are you all right?' Rafe asked as they ascended the stairs slower than he obviously would have liked.

'I'm fine,' she retorted, knowing his concern had less to do with her and more to do with the welfare of his unborn child. 'Just don't stick a pin in me or I might explode.' And while his low laugh irritated her, she was still grateful for his support as she made her way up the long sweeping stairway to the first floor.

The radiographers had set up their equipment in one of the unused rooms not far from her own, turning a bedchamber fit for a queen into a suite filled with the latest in medical technology. She blinked as she took it all in. Never before had she been in the position of having a doctor, let alone specialists, come to her—to ensure privacy, Rafe had told her, and she could understand that, although part of her wondered whether he thought there was a risk she might bolt if she had the chance to visit Velatte City.

Would she bolt, she wondered as she dutifully changed out of the clothes Rafe's minions had chosen for her into the robe they'd provided? Nothing of Rafe's plans to wed her had yet been announced, nobody knew who she was, and in the cover of the harbour city, unknown and unannounced, there was always the chance she'd be able to slip the palace guard and make her way to the port and secure a ticket to somewhere.

Away from Montvelatte and Rafe, at least she would have a fighting chance of thinking straight. Already her resolve was wavering, her determination not to be steamrolled into a wedding she didn't want dangerously slipping.

Which made no sense at all. She knew marriage could falter without love to bind the couple together; her own parents' marriage had taught her that.

Although at least her mother had wanted to marry.

Sienna hadn't even been asked the question.

'Are you ready?'

Rafe's voice broke her from her reverie and she allowed herself a wistful smile. *'Are you ready?'* was about the most romantic this wedding proposal was going to get.

Moments later she was on the stretcher draped in towels with her gown raised and her naked abdomen exposed. Soothing voices explained the procedure and assured her everything would be all right before cool jelly tickled as it was spread over her belly. She felt the pressure of the sensor sliding over her skin and for the very first time considered what might happen if something was wrong.

Sienna hadn't asked for this baby, hadn't wanted it or the marriage that Rafe assumed must go hand in hand with its existence. But if something was wrong with the baby, if he wasn't getting the package deal he was expecting, there was every likelihood he wouldn't want her any more.

Just for a moment, just a fraction of a moment, she almost let herself wish for the worst.

It hit her unexpectedly then, a hitherto unknown maternal guilt that she could be so cruel to her unborn child, tumbling and crashing over her in a wave that had her clamping her eyes tightly shut as she tried to blot out the possibility that something could be wrong. Because none of this was the baby's fault. She had no right to wish away this brand new speck of life just to solve her own problems. No right at all.

And suddenly, as the scanner slid across her skin, all that mattered was that her baby was healthy. Whatever else happened to her, it didn't matter, she would somehow cope.

But please, God, let her baby be healthy!

The radiographer seemed to be taking forever, biting her lip as she stared at the screen. She said something in her native Velattian-Italian language mix that had the obstetrician nodding as he studied the emerging pictures. She turned her head to see, but the screen was angled away from her, studied intently by the radiographer by her side and by both the specialist and Rafe at the foot of the bed. She strained to get higher. 'If you could lie still,' the radiographer encouraged, putting a hand to her shoulder.

'What's wrong,' Rafe asked her, his attention distracted from the screen.

'It's taking so long.'

The woman smiled and squeezed her arm. 'Don't worry,' she said, her accented words strangely soothing. 'Sometimes it takes a little time. As soon as we have a clear picture, I'll show you your *bambino*.'

Rafe joined her at the head of the bed, pulled up a chair and took her hand between his. 'You can't see there,' she warned, knowing how much he wanted to see the evidence of this child with his own eyes.

'So we'll see our baby together.' And the way he smiled at her raised goosebumps on her skin and hope in her heart. It seemed so real, like the smile a man would give a woman when she was carrying a child conceived in love. A smile so seemingly real it made her ache for all those real things she would never have—a real marriage, a man who wanted to marry her because he loved her and not for the baby she carried, a husband of her own choosing...

Sienna turned her head away and concentrated instead on the click and whirr of the machinery and the feel of the press of the device as it traced a path across her belly, the near-excruciating pressure against her over-full bladder all but banished by the feel of Rafe's hand around hers and the lazy stroke of his thumb.

She was asked to move a little to one side, then to the other, until after some time the radiographer appeared to find what she was looking for.

'Dottore Caporetto?' She looked over her shoulder then to the specialist, who was suddenly studying the screen intently, a frown gathering his already bushy brows, and a chill zipped down Sienna's spine.

Something *was* wrong.

Rafe's hand tightened around hers, as if he'd picked up on the vibe in the room as well. 'What is it?' he demanded in English. Then, *'C'e' qualcosa che non va, Dottore?'*

'Something you need to see,' he said, and the consultant angled the screen so that both of them had a clear view at last, into a murky sea of light and shadow where nothing made sense.

'I don't understand,' Sienna said. She'd known her baby would be tiny at this stage but she'd expected to see something recognizable, not this unreadable blur. 'What is it?'

The specialist said something to Rafe she didn't understand but she heard Rafe's sharp intake of breath, felt his withdrawal as he pushed himself back in his chair, and she feared the worst.

The specialist's face turned into a broad smile at Rafe's reaction, before he turned his attentions to her, patting her on the ankle. *'Va tutto benissimo. Auguri signorina, lei aspetta gemelli.'*

She shook her head and looked at Rafe who suddenly looked as shell-shocked as she felt. 'I don't understand. What's wrong? What's happening?'

'Ah, excuse me, please,' the *dottore* said, looking truly contrite as he pointed to twin smudges on the screen. 'In my excitement I forgot my manners. But you have my heartiest congratulations, *signorina*. It appears you are expecting twins.'

CHAPTER SEVEN

RAFE peered at the screen and at the two dark smudges in a
sea of light, smudges that proved beyond doubt he would
become a father not just once but twice over in a few short
months from now, a feeling of pride so huge in his chest that
he wanted to howl like the Beast of Iseo itself. What fortune
had brought Sienna to the island? Providence couldn't have
dealt him a better hand.

'Twins?' he heard her say, her voice shaky as if she couldn't
believe the news herself. 'It can't be…'

He lifted her hand then and pressed his lips against it. 'We
will marry as soon as possible,' he said. 'There can be no delay.'

Rafe took her to dinner that night, insisting they celebrate the
news, in a harbour-front restaurant where a private room fur-
nished with gilt mirrors and lush curtains had been set up for
them on an upstairs terrace that overlooked the lights of the
harbour front and the marina. It was the first time she'd been
to Velatte City, and she loved its vibrancy and colour and the
handsome people, their features a blend of the best the
Mediterranean could offer.

Carmelina had proven her worth as Sienna's wardrobe
manager, selecting without hesitation a gown shaded from

lilac through to a rich jewel-shade of amethyst that sat snug over Sienna's bustline before falling in soft, almost toga-like folds to the floor. With her hair coiled in wide ringlets and gathered up behind her head loosely for the ends to trail down, she almost felt like a Greek goddess. The way Rafe looked at her almost made her believe it.

Even so, the way he'd dressed made her wish she'd taken even more care. In a dark tuxedo and crisp white shirt he was magnificent, the Lombardi-crested cufflinks at his wrists, a burgundy tie at his throat. He looked like a man who had everything he wanted in the world, and if there was one tiny pang of regret about this whole celebration, it was that she knew that the babies she was carrying were a large part of it.

But she'd done a lot of thinking about those babies herself today, and a lot of it centered around her fears for what might happen if she did marry Rafe, and the quality of life she could offer them if she didn't.

One baby she believed she could cope with. She'd have to get a nanny, but she made decent money when she could fly. It would be hard to be a single mother, but at a stretch she would cope. Women did, all around the world, every day. Why couldn't she?

But knowing she was carrying twins had changed things, had tipped the balance. What kind of life could she offer them? What hope had she of being able to afford their care while she worked and what hope of giving them the family life they deserved? Would they grow up resenting her because she could not give them the lifestyle they would have had with their father?

But marriage without love? The one thing she feared more than anything.

How could he ask it of her?

They sat enjoying their entrées; a rare kind of peace descended on them as if Rafe too was deep in thought, while the vibrant waterfront buzzed below and the warm breeze tugged at her hair. Violin music drifted up from the main restaurant downstairs, gypsy music that was filled with life and hope and passion.

The first hint of the helicopter making its way across the harbour snared Sienna's attention like a magnet, even before the *whump* of the rotors became noticeable, and a familiar yearning surged anew. She followed its spotlight-lit path across the harbour, to where it landed atop one of the palace-like casinos lining the foreshore. She sighed as it landed. God, she missed flying, missed the feeling of soaring through the air like a bird, or skimming across the water like an insect. Missed the endless sky.

'What made you become a pilot?'

Sienna turned back to him, thinking it was odd that she was having his babies, that he fully intended to marry her, and yet they knew so very little about each other. 'The only thing I inherited from my father,' she started, 'was a love for travel. We lived on his boat my first few years, travelling the world, stopping in ports anywhere and everywhere. Until it was time for me to go to school and we dropped anchor in Gibraltar.'

'Sounds like a wonderful childhood.'

She gave a brief, harsh laugh, the sound of her father's constant taunts loud in her ears. 'I suppose it could have been.'

'It wasn't?'

'My father never wanted me. Always blamed me for ruining his life, for giving him responsibilities and putting an end to his wanderlust days. Ironic that I should inherit his love of travel, in that case, don't you think?'

Across the table, Rafe frowned, looking thoughtful. 'But boats never appealed?'

'God, no! Not after… Well, not after that. I used to lie on

the deck and watch the birds wheeling above. I used to imagine myself up there with them, it was the only way I could see to escape...' Her words trailed off. She'd said too much, revealed far too much of herself. She picked up her glass, swirling the sparkling water. 'Anyway, that's the dreary story of why I became a pilot.'

'No,' he said, squeezing her hand. 'Not dreary. Interesting. They must be proud of you.'

She looked out over the harbour and breathed in the smell of the sea and salt, finding a memory that brought a smile to her face. 'Mum was. She was ever so proud when I got my licence.' She turned and saw the question in his eyes. 'She died a few years back.'

'And your father?'

She shrugged. 'I don't know. I haven't seen him for years. He stayed in Gibraltar. We left.'

'I'm sorry,' he said.

'It's okay. Really. But can we talk about something a little more upbeat? Tell me about your sister. Where is she now?'

Rafe nodded as he sipped at his wine, and she couldn't tell if he was happy to accede to her request to change the topic, or just happy to think about his sister. 'She's fun. Where I was the serious one in the family, Marietta was always the hopeless romantic, the dreamer. She's a jewellery designer, and a seriously good one, now working in New Zealand. You'll like her, I know.'

She smiled. 'I think I will.'

A waiter came and topped up his wine, poured Sienna more lemon-flavoured mineral water and hovered just a moment too long to go unnoticed. Rafe looked up at him. 'Was there something else?'

'*Scusarmi, per favore,*' the red-faced waiter said with a nod, before rattling off a burst of language so fast and furious that Sienna had no hope of keeping up. Rafe answered, his smile

genuine as he rose from his seat to shake the man's hand, only
to be wrapped in an embrace that had the waiter looking mor-
tified with embarrassment before he bowed again and again
as he made his exit. *'Grazie. Grazie.'*

'What was that all about?'

Rafe gave a shrug as he sat down, as if it had been nothing.
'The waiter's father works as a teller at one of the casinos; his
mother is a cleaner there. He had been frightened that they
would all lose their jobs when they saw Carlo and Roberto
being arrested.'

'That's not all, though,' she said, sensing more in the
exchange from the odd word she'd picked up than he was
letting on. 'He was thanking you for coming back, wasn't he?'

He gazed out over the harbour, rather than at her, as if he
was uncomfortable with how much she had interpreted of the
exchange. 'Apparently so.'

She thought about the people who'd greeted and served
them tonight with smiles and warmth. She'd taken them for
granted—wouldn't they meet their Prince in such a way
anyway? But, looking back, there'd been a genuine warmth
in their welcome, as if the people of Montvelatte had
embraced their new Prince with joy. And Rafe's reaction to
the waiter's comments seemed to echo those sentiments.

'You really care about these people, don't you?'

He flicked his serviette back onto his lap. 'Does that
surprise you?'

She shrugged, embarrassed that she'd made so obvious her
prejudgment. 'But you never had anything to do with
Montvelatte before. You grew up in Paris, in exile with your
mother and sister.'

'You are right, of course. All I really knew was from my
mother's stories, or from the books she always encouraged us
to read. But being back here in Montvelatte, living here,

getting to know the people, it surprised me too how comfortable it felt. I am glad I decided to come back.' He reached across the table and wrapped one of her hands in his own, and she felt the sincerity of his words in his touch.

'Was there ever any doubt?' she asked, liking the way her hand felt in his, the way his fingers stroked the skin of her hand into sensual awareness. 'I thought you had decided that night, as soon as the reports came in, that this was your destiny.'

He shook his head. 'I wasn't planning to come at all—not at first. Not until Yannis called.' He broke off suddenly to explain. 'Yannis Markides, my business partner but more than that, my lifelong friend. It was Yannis who made me see sense. But when I did decide to come, it wasn't because I felt some inexplicable link with the island or its people.'

'Then why?'

His thumbs made lazy circles on her hand, lazy circles that sent busy signals vibrating through her veins. 'Two things. One part of me wanted to prove that a bastard son, the son his father had rejected, could make something of himself, could prove himself to be a worthy ruler.' He fixed her with eyes full of meaning. 'It seems that I, too, was blessed with a father who didn't want me.'

Sienna bristled under his gaze, not at all sure she was comfortable having something in common with him, let alone a reason to empathise with him. 'And the other?'

'Because of my mother. She loved her Mediterranean island home and hated being exiled like some criminal simply because she'd borne the Prince a bastard son and daughter. Do you understand? By coming back, I could try to make things right for her. That was my motivation. But I had no idea when I made that decision just how right it would come to feel.'

Sienna shivered, picking up on his use of past tense. His mother was dead. She recalled reading that in a magazine article after Rafe's coronation. But it hadn't occurred to her then that it was something else they shared.

She picked up her glass of water in her free hand, desperate for something to do to hide her confusion. She hated being wrong about things, hated knowing she'd made judgements based on assumptions that were misplaced. She'd assumed Rafe had embraced his new role because he'd imagined himself born to rule. Had believed it, considering the way he'd treated her. But given his story and the way the people here seemed to react to him, maybe she'd been wrong about that. Maybe he wasn't the beast she imagined him to be...

'I have something for you,' he said, interrupting her thoughts while he reached into his pocket.

She sat up straight, suddenly defensive, interlocking both hands under the table in case he was about to make some kind of engagement ring gesture. Despite their more civilized conversation tonight, and despite her shifting thoughts, she wasn't ready for anything like that yet, hoped that tonight wasn't about that. 'What is it?'

The ruby-red box looked worn, the velvet scuffed at the corners. 'It's my mother's favourite piece of jewellery. I thought you should have it.'

Sienna shook her head, while he pressed the box towards her until it would have been churlish not to raise her hands and accept it. 'But it was your mother's. Shouldn't it go to your sister?'

'Open it,' he urged. She gasped as the case snapped open, revealing the stunning jewels within, gemstones of every hue and shade, suspended at intervals from a diamond-set necklace.

'It's beautiful,' was her first reaction. 'I can't accept this,' was her second. But he was already on his feet, taking the necklace from its setting and fixing it at her throat. She put a hand to the precious piece, the jewels feeling heavy and cool against her skin, whereas the brush of his fingers felt warm at her throat, but all too light and all too brief.

He sat down again, the fire in the gems reflected in the flames in his eyes. 'They suit you.' And then, 'did I tell you how beautiful you look tonight?'

She dropped her eyes. 'Carmelina chose it.'

'It's not the dress,' he said. 'It's you. You look radiant.' He lifted his glass to her. 'Here's to you, my future bride, the mother of Montvelatte's future.'

She trembled, the responsibility of the title he'd just bestowed upon her feeling like a leaded weight. 'Look, Rafe, I haven't actually agreed to marry you yet.'

He frowned, her words clearly taking him off guard, before reaching over the table to take her hand. 'What choice do we have? Soon you will start to show. Do you want this marriage to look like some shotgun wedding?'

Like her parents' perchance? His words cut through the goodwill they'd built tonight like a scythe, sharp and deep, re-opening old wounds and laying them bare. 'If I *did* agree to marry you, why shouldn't it look that way, when that's exactly what it is?'

'I prefer to call it a marriage of convenience, for both of us.'

'And I call it like I see it. You may not be holding a shot-gun to my head, but you might as well be. What choice have you given me?'

Candlelight flickered in his dark eyes. 'I'm sorry. Maybe coming out tonight was premature and you are not yet ready to see sense.'

'As you are not yet ready to see my point of view!'

He sighed and leant back in his chair, throwing his napkin down onto the table. 'And what is your point of view? That you can go on your merry way carrying two royal babies and somehow continue your life as a helicopter pilot as if nothing had happened?' He cursed under his breath and stood, signalling to the waiter for the car to be brought around.

She remained exactly where she was and jagged her chin up higher. 'I don't know any more. Two babies—I just don't know. But I do know that whatever you call it, a marriage between us will have no chance of success while we remain virtual strangers. Look at our conversation tonight, we don't know the first thing about each other.'

For a moment his jaw looked so set she thought he might just turn and leave without her, and then he breathed out on a sigh and folded himself into his chair again, nodding. 'Si. You are right. I am rushing you. Would a month be long enough, do you think?'

He was giving her a month to decide? She rolled the proposal around in her head, looking for the catch but happy to take any concession going given the way she'd been railroaded up until now. 'That would certainly help.'

It did help. Rafe had Sebastiano rearrange his diary to free up his evenings over the course of the next week, taking her to the opera, to the opening of a play and countless magnificent dinners overlooking the lights of the city or the harbour or sometimes even both. They were photographed wherever they went, a buzz around them whenever they were spotted, and while Sienna knew there would be pictures in magazines and articles written about them, she wasn't uncomfortable with the attention. She'd made no commitment to him. She had her month and she had the time to get to know Rafe better.

At every event, Sienna was reminded of what it was that had put her under Rafe's spell from the very beginning. He could be so utterly charming, his attention focused one hundred per cent on her and her alone, to the exclusion of everything and everyone else. She'd missed that attention, especially lately. Missed the feeling that she was special for herself. And all the while he'd been the perfect gentleman, never pushing her for so much as a kiss, even though there were times she saw his need in a glance or in the tightness of his movements, like he was trying to keep it in check. She appreciated it. They'd known each other's bodies before they'd known the first thing about each other. Now they could redress the balance.

And at every outing she saw the people's reaction when they met their Prince. There was respect there, to be sure, but there was joy too as he mixed with his people, and a kind of elation lifted the crowd.

And she decided he was a good prince for Montvelatte.

They were just leaving an exhibition at an art gallery one day when it happened. A small crowd had assembled outside, cheering behind a cordon of palace guards as they made their exit. A small girl squirmed out from between a guard's legs and ran towards them carrying a hand-picked posy of flowers that she held up for Sienna to take, her dark eyes wide as if begging her to accept her gift. Sienna smiled and reached down. *'Grazie,'* she said, and the little girl beamed before throwing herself at Rafe's legs and wrapping her arms around them in a bear hug. A guard came closer, but Rafe shooed him away, instead picking up the small girl and hoisting her into his arms as he made his way to the crowd and her parents. *'Ringraziarla, la bella ragazza,'* and the child's smile widened before she threw her arms around his neck and kissed him on the cheek.

Sienna's grip had tightened around the posy, just as a band had twisted around her heart. He wasn't just a good prince. He would make a damn fine father as well.

Rafe was nothing like her own father. Though it wasn't as if he'd wanted children so much as heirs, at least he would never tell these babies that they'd ruined his life.

Was that enough?
Could she risk it?
She was almost tempted.

CHAPTER EIGHT

SIENNA sat in the library, a half-eaten sandwich and a forgotten cup of tea by her side, but it wasn't morning sickness curbing her appetite. Neither was it the Italian language study book, a handbook on royal protocol, and a short history of Montvelatte in twelve volumes that Sebastiano had so generously decided might be worth her while flicking through while Rafe was busy in Rome presenting his fiscal rescue package for Montvelatte to international financiers.

It was the parchment in her hand that had anger welling up inside her until there was space for nothing else. He'd given her a month, he'd said, to give them a chance to get to know each other, but the date on the invitation in front of her told her nothing of the sort.

She would become Rafe's bride and the new Princess of Montvelatte in less than two weeks. Rafe certainly wasn't wasting any time inducting her into the family firm or in waiting for her to make up her own mind. Neither was he wasting any time keeping her informed.

But, then, why would he? He still hadn't asked her to marry him. Simply taken it for granted that she would fall in with his plans.

And, damn it, why the hell should she? She was pregnant

with his babies, but that was where his interest in having her as his wife began and ended. She'd never been on that list of potential wives Sebastiano had been scouting, and she never would have been considered but for one unprotected moment and an unplanned pregnancy that had resulted.

And until he'd discovered her condition, he'd been prepared to let her leave the island so he could resume his search for a princess. He'd made it clear that he was willing to bed her and that was all.

She'd only been promoted to the top by default. By an accident. A mistake.

It wasn't good enough.

It wasn't *enough*.

Sienna let her hands drop into her lap and squeezed her eyes shut. What was she thinking—that this marriage might work, that if she and Rafe got to know each other properly, they might make a go of it? Because she could marry him and still end up with nothing. There were no guarantees. And babies simply weren't enough to hold a marriage together. She was living proof of that. Only love could cement a marriage together—love on both sides.

Once upon a time, in a bed in what seemed for ever ago, she thought she'd found those first magical stirrings of love. But she'd been wrong. Her sense of wonder at a wave of new-found feelings had been misplaced. Apparently it had only ever been about the sex.

And when she'd arrived on the island and was prevented from leaving, that had all been about the sex as well. Rafe had wanted to use her—and discard her—all over again.

And soon, unless she found another solution, they would be married, and still love had nothing to do with it.

Marriage. How could she do it? How could she marry a man she didn't love and who didn't love her, a man who saw her as either his personal sex toy or his personal incubator and to hell with her career, a career he was only too happy to throw on the trash heap in his pursuit of his own goals? A man who lied to her and who gave her no choice?

How could it ever work?

'Sebastiano said you wanted to see me.'

Sienna jumped, so deep in thought that she hadn't heard Rafe's approach. He obviously hadn't been back long. He was tugging at his tie, still wearing a dark suit and crisp white shirt that accentuated his olive skin. A five o'clock shadow that made designer stubble look contrived dusted his strong jawline and gave him an almost piratical appearance. How could anyone look so good no matter what they wore?

Or didn't wear, for that matter.

She dropped her eyes, trying to focus on the invitation in her hands, and why she'd been so angry, instead of the thought of the skin under that suit, skin she'd be seeing a lot more of if this damned marriage took place as planned. And that thought didn't help her burning face one bit.

Sienna stood and waved the paper in her hand, hoping he would assume that it was the reason for the heightened colour in her cheeks. 'You told me I had a month to decide what I was doing.'

'Did I?'

'You know you did. At that dinner the night of the scan. You said we had a month to get to know each other.'

'And your problem is?'

'Today I find this!' She thrust the invitation under his face so he had no choice but to take it, giving it a brief glance.

'You're not happy with the invitations?'

'I'm not happy with the date! Look at it. You said we had a month to get to know each other, a month to make up my mind before any date was set, but this says we are to be married in less than two weeks. You lied to me!'

'No! I never said you had a month to make up anything of the sort. I asked you if a month was enough to get to know each other and you said it was. Which was fortunate, as the wedding date had already been set.'

Blood pounded at her temples. 'You knew the date had been set and you didn't tell me? When you knew I thought I had a month to make up my mind?'

'And haven't we been doing that, Sienna?' he said, coming closer until there was only a hands breadth between them, and fielding her question with one of his own. 'Haven't we been getting to know each other? I thought you'd enjoyed our evenings out together?'

She could feel the heat emanating from him, but it was the scent of him that threatened to scramble her brain. A scent she hadn't realized how much she'd missed these last three days. With a strength of will fuelled by her anger, she spun away, out of range.

'That's not the point. You led me to believe that I could make up my own mind, that it would be my decision. And it will be my decision. I will not be railroaded into marrying you. I want these invitations stopped.'

'I'm afraid it's too late for that. Sebastiano informs me that they've already gone out.'

'But I haven't said I'll marry you.'

He shrugged. 'And now you don't have to.'

'How dare you!' She was sick of his arrogance. Sick of his attitude, sick of having all her reservations thrust aside as if they counted for nothing. 'And what of my life? I'm a helicopter pilot, Rafe, not a princess!'

'In less than two weeks, you will be both.'

She scoffed. 'And you would have me believe I can keep my job?'

He slammed the invitation down on the table. 'Don't be

ridiculous. I can't have my wife running joy flights around the Mediterranean. You will have work here. As Montvelatte's Princess. As mother of our children.'

'I worked hard to become a pilot! I worked damned hard to get to where I am now and not by flying joy flights. How can you expect me to throw it all away to fall in with your plans?'

Rafe sighed, pinching the bridge of his nose with his fingers. 'But don't you see, you have no alternative. Your flying career crunched to a halt the minute you became pregnant with twins.'

'And who damn well got me pregnant!'

'Guilty,' he acceded, making his way to a sideboard and pouring himself a healthy slug of Scotch that he held up in mock toast to her. 'And for my sins I will marry you. Surely you can't ask for more than that.' He threw the glass back, draining half the contents. 'Now, if that was all? I do have some work to attend to.'

He was already turning to go when she stepped forward and grabbed the sleeve of his jacket. 'Don't dismiss me like some minion with a petty grievance.'

His eyes glittered with an icy cold ferocity as his eyes scanned upwards from the hand on his forearm to her face. 'Clearly, that would be a mistake on my part. But let me make one thing patently clear. We are getting married on the date printed on that invitation, whether you like it or not.'

'And if I refuse?'

'Then I will throw you over my shoulder and carry you to the altar, if that's what it takes.'

'Why not just club me over the head and drag me there and prove to the world what a beast you really are?'

A muscle popped in his jaw, the fires in his eyes growing even colder. 'What a tempting prospect. I must keep that in mind. But rest assured, this wedding will happen. Whether or not you embrace the concept is entirely up to you.'

* * *

What was her problem? Rafe pulled off his tie and tugged at the buttons at his neck as he strode into his bookshelf-lined study. Couldn't Sienna see it was the only way? *Merda*, it solved everybody's problems in one neat package.

He threw himself into the high-back leather chair behind his desk, took one look at the untidy pile of reports and files sitting on his desk waiting for his attention and swung around to stare out the windows over the neat lines of the courtyard garden and to the azure sea beyond the cliff walls instead. He gazed out of the window, unseeing, knowing he should be tackling the paperwork. With the question of continuing the Lombardi line so neatly wrapped up, he should have been able to spend more time on the more pressing financial problems that threatened to undermine Montvelatte's economy, and helping with unravelling the intricate web of companies, dummy companies and trusts that his half-brothers had established in an attempt to ensure that the ultimate beneficiaries of the stolen casino funds would never be discovered.

They had been, but with the mess they had left behind, it would take time to get Montvelatte back on a sound financial footing.

But instead of spending time on the problem, he'd had to pander to Sienna's wishes, spending evenings with her, making her think he was going along with her wish to get to know him better. It hadn't been that onerous, surprisingly enough, the woman he'd chosen because she was pregnant with his babies, and because of how she could pleasure him in bed, turning out to be an unexpected success with the crowds.

So what was her problem? She'd enjoyed their time together, and he'd had no doubt that a month would be all it would take to convince her that marriage did not have to be the disaster she coloured it.

It had been going so well until she had spotted that invitation. How the hell had she got hold of that?

But what was worse, he'd told her that he'd carry her to the altar if she refused to marry him, and at the time he'd meant every word. Although with the cameras and the guests and the world watching, that was never on the cards. He needed her to walk down that aisle of her own free will.

Christo, but he wanted her there. Over the last few days in Rome he'd missed her more than he'd expected, and the idea of returning to her had held more and more appeal. She might not come with the pedigree that Sebastiano was so hopeful of securing for Montvelatte's Princess, but her fresh beauty could only give the monarchy a boost, and in terms of a partner, he was much happier to have someone he knew he was compatible with in bed than the pick of some highly strung finishing school graduates. *Dio*, but how he was looking forward to renewing that part of their relationship.

He swore under his breath as his thoughts turned to rock-hard reality. He had work to do, and the last thing he needed was to feel that familiar tightening in his groin.

He swivelled around in the chair and let his eyes slide over the piles of paperwork requiring his attention before this evening's dinner meeting with Montvelatte's Minister of Finance.

And then he remembered the wounded look in Sienna's hazel eyes as he'd stormed out of the room and instantly his priorities changed. For as much as she liked to call him the Beast of Iseo, he needed her to walk up that aisle willingly…

Rafe found her sitting on the side of the pool, her filmy floral skirt hiked up above her knees as she dipped her calves in the water. She looked beautiful like that, leaning back on her hands and making circles with her feet that spun with light through the water. Beautiful and yet, oh, so sad.

'Am I disturbing you?'

Sienna glanced briefly in his direction and then away. 'I thought you had work to do,' she said, but not before he'd caught the flash of surprise. Surprise and something else that had skated across the surface of her eyes too quickly to pin down, but enough to encourage him. She was angry, but there was something else there as well. That was a start.

'Work can wait. I needed some fresh air and thought, now that it's approaching evening, a walk on the cliff path would be good. Have you done that yet?'

She shook her head, sitting straight up now and sweeping her hands clean.

'Would you like to?'

She blinked once, suspiciously, and then again less so, and finally she gave the briefest of nods. 'Thank you.' She swung her legs out of the pool and reached for a towel, but he was already there with it. Their hands met as he passed it to her, and she jerked away, as quickly and gracefully as a startled gazelle.

'Come,' he said, once she'd slipped on her sandals. 'This way.'

It was still warm, but the sun was dipping lower in the sky and the scent of a thousand wild herbs and flowers played on the fresh sea air as he led her, neither of them speaking, around the Castello wall and onto the narrow path that wended its way around the headland. Low scrubby bush hugged the sides of the path, tiny pink flowers jostling with each other in the light early-evening breeze.

In the distance the shard of rock that was Iseo's Pyramid thrust savagely into the sky, with its ever-changing cloud of sea birds wheeling and circling its heights, and from this angle it looked even more dangerous, as if slicing through the water like an enormous black fin. They stopped to look at it at one point, where an enormous chair had been carved out of ancient rock.

'Tell me about the legend,' Sienna asked, standing in front of it, hugging her arms around herself as she looked across the sea to the rocky islet.

Rafe studied her face—the blandness of her expression, the tightness around her eyes. There was a vulnerability about her this evening that he hadn't seen before, almost as if she'd lost her fight and had become resigned to her fate.

He didn't like it. He liked her passive even less than he did when she argued with him. At least then she showed the passion for which he knew she was capable.

She turned her head then, her eyes questioning, and reluctantly he turned his eyes away and towards the chunk of rock she seemed to find so fascinating. 'It was the making of Montvelatte,' he told her. 'The waters are treacherous around the Pyramid; many ships have come to grief in trying to negotiate a passage between the mainland and the island. Blown off course, the pyramid was almost a magnet. Many went down. Many men died.'

'And the beast? How did that story come about?'

'There were always stories, always a suggestion that there was more to the dangers of the Pyramid than an iceberg carved from rock. And then, on a night with no moon and a savage storm, legend has it that a vessel carrying riches from the east to Genoa was blown onto the rocks and sliced in two. One man miraculously survived, only to witness the breaking apart of his vessel and the deaths of all those he'd sailed with. It was he who first saw the beast when lightning lit up the sky. The beast was standing atop the Pyramid and howling into the storm, the bloodied remains of one of his fellow sailors in its maw. That man was Iseo.'

Alongside him she shivered, and he would have reached

out an arm to bring her close, but he knew she wasn't shivering with the cold, and he sensed his arm around her shoulders would not be welcome. 'What happened to him?'

'He clung to some debris and made it here. Eventually he went mad, if he weren't already. But not before everyone had heard the story. And believed it.'

'What a horrible story.'

'Though fortunate for Montvelatte.'

She looked up at him. 'How so?'

He shrugged. 'Some enterprising pirate decided it was easier to make a living by exacting a toll from passing ships to guarantee them safe passage past the Beast, rather than bother with attacking them. It was only the ones who refused to pay that he was forced to attack.'

'Oh, my,' she said, with what sounded suspiciously like a laugh. 'Very entrepreneurial.'

And he laughed at her unexpected response, suddenly glad he'd swapped a mountain of work on his desk for a walk in the fresh air with a woman who continued to surprise him at every turn.

A woman already pregnant with his seed.

A woman who would soon be his wife.

And once again the beast inside him swelled like it had been fed. This would work, he knew in his gut that this marriage would work. *One way or another.* He just had to make her see it.

A noise interrupted them, and Rafe cursed himself for not turning off his cell phone. No doubt Sebastiano was checking up on him, his schedule thrown by Rafe's spur-of-the-moment change of plans. The caller ID confirmed his suspicions before Sebastiano's gently chiding voice reminded him of a meeting he hadn't forgotten at all. Simply wished he could.

Rafe pretended to listen while he watched Sienna turn her

focus on the ancient stone seat, running her hands over the weathered contours of the rock. He followed their progress, watching her fingers trailing across the surface, hit with the sudden memory of how those same fingers had felt dancing across his skin, her nails biting into his flesh when he'd turned his attentions to a place that had made her gasp and curl her fingers deeper.

And suddenly his body ached to feel the curl and bite of them in his flesh again.

He watched her move, absorbing the gentle sway of her hips and the sweet curve of her neck into his being as one absorbed sunshine.

How long would he have to wait? Until their marriage night? The doctor had told him there was no reason they should not resume a normal sex life, but he'd been assuming they'd had a normal sex life, when all they'd shared had been just one night. Definitely not normal. And definitely not enough.

And while he intended to remedy that the first chance he got, right now was hardly the best time.

One step at a time. He wouldn't rush her or she'd consider it just another ploy. As much as he preferred her passion to the passive sadness he'd witnessed in her most recently, the last thing he needed to give her was another reason to fight him before the wedding. That wasn't the kind of passion he wanted. Once she was legally his, there would be plenty of opportunity for passion.

But the best part of two more weeks? It would be agony.

Sebastiano's voice had long died away when she looked up and caught his gaze on her, her hands halting their exploration as her eyes widened in surprise. She swept her hands away from the rock, as if embarrassed. 'The stone is so beautiful.'

'It's called Vincenzo's throne,' he said, drawing up so close behind her that the breeze, so usually filled with the perfume of wild flowers and aromatic leaves, was laced with the warm scent of her. 'After the first Prince of Montvelatte. Nobody knows who carved the seat or when, but it was right here that Montvelatte first became a Principality.'

She flicked a nervous glance over her shoulder, as if surprised by how close he was, before spinning away and turning her attention back to the seat, running a hand along its surface. 'I was intending to read about that today,' she said. 'How did it come about?'

He allowed himself a smile as she feigned complete and total interest in the ancient relic. But he could tell by the rapid rise and fall of her chest and the slashes of colour on her cheeks that she felt it too, this hunger to renew their intimate acquaintance.

Two weeks? *Dio*, he hoped not.

'It was way back in the fourteenth century,' he began, as he watched her take her place on the wide throne, testing the seat before venturing to turn her eyes towards him again. 'A vessel carrying the royal family of Karpenthia was on its way to Genoa. At that time Karpenthia was a rich power in the north of Africa, built where the camel trade routes met the sea, while Velatte City was a seedy place of prostitutes and pirates and assorted runaways. But the King's daughter was ill with fever and close to death, so they pulled into harbour. It was a brave thing that they did, risking the lives of everyone on board, but they had no choice.'

Her eyes widened, her interest obviously piqued. 'What happened?'

'A man came forward from the crowd that came to meet the vessel. When he saw who was on board, he promised to cure the girl, and so they carried her to a hut, where his grandmother, an old crow of a woman reported to have magical healing powers, concocted a remedy made from the local herbs gathered from the side of these very cliffs.'

'The old woman saved her.'

Rafe nodded. 'The King was so grateful he drafted up a deed declaring Montvelatte a Principality in its own right, with the grandson, the man who'd promised to cure the princess, its first Prince. That man was Vincenzo Lombardi. Two years later the princess returned and became his first Princess of Montvelatte.'

'She married Vincenzo, to live amongst pirates and prostitutes?'

He shrugged as he leaned back against one arm of the stone seat. 'Legend has it that it was a great love match, and one that changed the course of Montvelatte forever. Apparently the original part of the Castello, built on the remains of ancient fortresses going back over the centuries, was his tribute to her.'

'You sound like you don't really believe it.'

'Maybe I'm a cynic, but I suspect that Vincenzo wouldn't have been backward about naming his price for saving the King's daughter.'

'But then why would the King have brought his daughter back once they'd got away? Why couldn't the story be true?'

'It's just a fairy tale. It doesn't work that way.'

'It's a legend.' She shook her head, so that her hair rippled about her head, dancing on the light. 'But why shouldn't it also be true? What better way to start a new nation?'

But that would mean loving someone could be a good thing!

He turned away, suddenly not wanting her to see his eyes. She had a way sometimes of piercing his shell and seeing inside him, of reaching into the deepest parts of him, the hidden parts of him, and of asking the questions no one else dared. Because no one else knew how he'd felt growing up and feeling his mother's pain at being an outcast, discarded like a pair of worn out shoes.

'Don't waste your time on love,' he remembered his mother softly singing as he'd lain tucked up in bed while she rocked his sister to sleep, crooning the words over and over like a lullaby. *'Don't lose your heart. Stay strong, my baby, be strong.'*

And so he'd grown up determined to be strong and to make it on his own, determined to prove to the world that a title meant nothing, that it was what one made of oneself that counted.

And given the mess his half-brothers had made of things, he had more reason to believe that than ever. He stared out to sea and to the black peak that was Iseo's Pyramid and wondered about the beast that reputedly lived there. Who needed a beast when so much darkness resided in one's own heart?

'So the pirate island becomes a Principality,' he heard her say. 'Surely the neighbouring countries objected?'

Rafe turned to see her looking up at the castle, pushing a few wayward strands of hair from her face with her hands. He bit back on a growl, forcing himself to remember his determination to wait for her. Did she have any idea how that action lifted her breasts, displaying their outline to perfection?

Sienna let her arms drop and swivelled around, and he had to prise his eyes back up to hers to meet her gaze.

'The royal families of both France and Italy held the Karpenthian King in high regard. And while neither had been interested in the island until then, content to leave it to the pirates and criminals, they imposed the condition that only a Lombardi could take the crown, that if the bloodline was broken, so too was the agreement.'

'And that's why you had to come back.'

'That's why.'

'What would have happened if you hadn't?'

'Then the pressure would have been on Marietta, as heir presumptive, to take the throne. But she's never wanted it, her links with the island even more tenuous than mine. Besides,

I couldn't put that kind of pressure on her, and I know my mother would never have forgiven me for walking away and allowing Montvelatte to lose its status as a Principality. Its land and wealth, what's left of it, for the taking.'

'By Italy?'

'Or France, depending on who makes the stronger case. Already legal teams in a dozen capital cities throughout Europe are arguing over the details, just in case.' She nodded, and he watched her stoop to pick a flower from one of the many low-growing bushes around, holding the shell-pink flower up to her nose and breathing in its fragrance. He didn't tell her that the update he'd received today had suggested that developments on the island were being keenly watched, the identity of the Prince's apparent new escort and rumours of a royal pregnancy being investigated.

Neither did he tell her of the report he'd received from the security check Sebastiano had had run on Sienna's background. And one thing shone out like a beacon. There had been no other men in her life around the time he had pursued her, or for several months before. He was the only one, confirming all he'd believed and more.

More reason then ever to get married and quickly.

They continued together, circling around the high walls of the Castello to where the hill dropped away into a steep valley behind. Terraced vineyards lined the slopes, leading down to a narrow river that curved away to the harbour where the buildings of Velatte City huddled along the shoreline. He heard her gasp as she took in the beauty before them, as mountain-bred vines gave way to the familiar white architecture of the city, which ended in a row of casinos, each more magnificent than the next, lining the white-fringed harbour far below.

'It's so beautiful from up here,' she said. 'I had no idea this path even existed.' And he felt a stab of remorse that he'd kept her largely locked away within the Castello walls, expecting her to be entertained with dusty books and language lessons when he wasn't parading her in front of the world's paparazzi, with not a hint of sharing with her the real beauty of the island that would now be her home.

And now her eyes sparkled, her smile broad as she surveyed the world over which she would soon rule by his side, and he couldn't help but take her hand in his own as she stood there, marvelling at the view. Her eyes briefly darted to his, but she didn't pull away, and he moved closer by her side, pointing out the peaks of craggy hills just visible behind the other side of the valley. 'The island extends another fifteen kilometres beyond Velatte City to the south. Predominantly small villages situated amongst vineyards and olive groves or on the coast. And, of course, like any Mediterranean island, you will find the obligatory hotel resorts, although Montvelatte's main tourism thrust has been via the casinos.'

'So beautiful,' she repeated. He watched her as her gaze scanned from one spectacular end of the valley to the other, her free hand held up to shield her eyes from the setting sun while the silken fabric of her skirt shifted and rippled around her legs in the barely there breeze.

'Without a doubt.'

And she turned towards him, her lips slightly parted, her eyes questioning.

'You could be happy,' he said, 'living here.'

And the lights in her eyes dimmed a little then. 'Rafe,' she said softly, so softly he felt his name on her breath even as he read it on her lips. Lips that beckoned him and drew him closer. Lips that made him ache with wanting her.

She shook her head, the barest, almost imperceptible movement from side to side, which he refused to accept as meaning she didn't want his kiss. Not when her eyes gave him a different message and her lips were already parted and ready for him.

And so he cupped her warm cheek with his hand, and on a tiny track, below the Castello Montvellate and above the magnificent sweep of valley below, his world shrank to just one woman, and one moment in time.

And that moment held its breath and hovered between them, shimmering with intensity as he lowered his mouth to hers. She shuddered into the kiss, and he slid his hand around the back of her neck to steady her, weaving his fingers into her hair, the taste of her flooding his senses and firing his blood.

She tasted of sunshine and vanilla, of warmth and woman, and the way her lips moved under his told him he was not the only one involved in this kiss. She was there, every part of her. She was his. He gathered her to him with his free arm, finding that sweet spot in the curve of her spine that brought her fully against his aching length.

She gasped into his mouth but she didn't fight, didn't move away. Instead she settled even closer, the subtle squirm of her hips a sweet agony that he poured into his kiss, to her lips, to her cheeks, to her eyes. And everywhere he kissed just fuelled the need that had been building ever since she'd stepped out of that helicopter, a need that refused to be compartmentalized and set aside.

I want you, he wanted to whisper, while his teeth nuzzled at her lobe. She trembled as if he'd said the words and threw her head back, forcing her breasts harder against his chest, so that he ached to free them and reacquaint himself with their satin perfection, longed to draw their pebbled peaks deep into his mouth.

Instead, he dragged in a lungful of air, fighting the urge to take her, right here, right now, on this lonely path high above the city, knowing it was madness when the paparazzi made an art form of lying in wait and holding out for the perfect shot, and yet still having to fight the beast for supremacy.

She'd already made him wait so long—*too long*—but soon, he told himself, encouraged by her participation, there was no doubt in his mind that very soon he would have her again.

Hesitatingly, reluctantly, he slowed the kiss, drawing back as he loosened his arms around her. She opened her eyes, and he saw her bewilderment, sensed her disappointment and very nearly changed his mind.

'We should get back,' he said, wishing she would argue, wishing she would demand that he stay and kiss her again, needing a damned good reason to let her go. 'I have a meeting I'm already late for,' he said, trying to convince himself. 'Besides which, we don't want you catching a chill.'

And before his eyes her back seemed to stiffen, her expression cooling so quickly that he ached to turn back the clock and take back his words.

'Of course,' she said, tucking the hair that had so recently coiled thick and silkily around his fingers behind her ears as she turned away. 'I'd hate to catch a chill.'

CHAPTER NINE

SHE was a fool. Forty-eight hours later, that was the only explanation Sienna could come up with as she paced to and fro under the dappled shade of the vine-covered terrace, her various text books lying open and abandoned on the table nearby.

Two nights ago she'd gone to sleep—eventually—with the memories of that cliff-path walk playing through her mind. They'd walked together along a cliff top path breathing fresh sea air scented with a myriad different wild flowers and herbs, and then he'd wrapped her hand in his as they'd gazed out over a view that was to die for. And then he'd kissed her, and the defensive walls she'd built around herself, and that he'd been unsettling ever since he'd found her poolside and asked her to walk with him, had been rocked apart.

He hadn't pushed, hadn't demanded a thing from her, and yet one simple kiss and all her defenses had been ready to crumble, like some impressionable teenager on her first date.

And for a moment there—just one tiny moment, when they'd looked out over the view and he'd asked her if she could be happy here—she'd almost imagined that he'd meant it, that he cared that she might be happy, and that he wanted her to stay. In that precious moment, and in the kiss that had followed, she'd felt the barriers she'd put up around herself tremble and shake, and her emotions tilt and slide within their unsteady walls...

And then, with one simple line, he'd firmed her emotions and her resolve. He hadn't wanted her to catch a chill. The temperature must have been in the mid-twenties Celcius with no more than a slight onshore breeze, and he had been worried about her catching a chill.

And his concern hadn't been for her benefit.

She'd ceased being someone who merited concern in her own right when she'd become his own personal incubator.

Of course he wanted her to be happy here—he needed to know the mother of his children wasn't about to take off unexpectedly, with or without them—but he'd done nothing to ensure her happiness. Merely expected it, just like he expected her to marry him.

Sienna looked wistfully over to the vacant helipad, wondering what she'd be up to and where she'd be flying now if she wasn't trapped here on this island. And then she remembered why she was trapped and that she probably wouldn't be flying anyway, and her heart sank even lower.

She turned her eyes in the direction of the books that lay open and accusing in front of her, and she questioned herself why it was that she was going along with everything as though she'd agreed to this marriage.

Maybe her work options were limited, at least while any shred of morning sickness remained, but after finding out how Rafe had betrayed her by continuing to plan a wedding she hadn't agreed to, why the hell was she still here? It wasn't as if one kiss on their walk that night was going to make Rafe forget the tiny detail she was pregnant and want to marry her for her own sake.

Fat chance.

He'd kissed her, and she'd felt—at least, she'd thought she'd felt—that there was something there, some hint of caring for her, and it had taken her unawares and she'd kissed him back.

But that faint hope had turned to nothing more than dust when he'd turned around and urged her to go back inside for the sake of her unborn babies.

Was it too much to hope that he might actually care for her for her own sake? Was that really too much to ask?

What kind of man would expect her to be able to marry someone who didn't love her?

She gazed out over the view, the blue sea and azure sky totally wasted on her. She'd promised herself it wouldn't happen. Years of watching the pain her mother felt, loving a man who'd been forced into a marriage he didn't want, years of watching her parents' marriage stagnate and fester until it had imploded in grand style, had convinced her that she could never marry a man who didn't love her.

And years of bearing the guilt that she'd been the one who'd forced her parents into a pointless marriage had made her more determined than ever that any child of hers would never be forced to bear that same burden.

'If it weren't for you, I could have made something of my life.'
'If it weren't for you, I wouldn't have a care in the world.'
'If it weren't for you...'

How many times, in how many different ways, had her father made her realize that everything wrong in his life was all down to her? All because he'd been forced into a marriage he didn't want. All because of an unplanned pregnancy.

Rafe might be a different man from her father, but his motives were hardly pure. She couldn't bear for her children to realize they hadn't been born in love, to know that their father had only wanted them for political purposes.

She couldn't bear it.

If she had to marry anyone, there was only one way it might

happen, only one way it could possibly work. If she had to marry anyone, he was damn well going to have to love her first.

Which meant that she couldn't just wait for Rafe to have the time to notice her. Whatever had motivated Rafe into taking her for a cliff-top stroll last night—probably guilt that she'd found out his duplicity—he'd not bothered to seek her company today. She knew work was his priority right now. She knew and understood that his focus was on getting Montvelatte back onto a sound financial footing, but it was also clear that if she wanted him to fall in love with her, then she was going to have to try something more than a friendly conversation.

Sienna picked up the nearest phone and dialed the number that she knew would put her instantly in contact with Sebastiano's office. The phone was answered almost immediately, the transfer to Sebastiano taking only moments longer.

'Where can I catch up with Rafe tonight?'

'Prince Raphael should not be expected back at the Castello before eleven p.m., possibly later.'

'And where can I find him before then?'

There was hesitation at the end of the line. 'Prince Raphael is currently attending a meeting of the casino finance managers at Casino de Velatte after which he's due at a recital in the casino's Crystal Ballroom.'

'Perfect,' said Sienna, already mentally trawling through the myriad evening gowns that hung in her endless closets. 'Can you take me there?'

This time the pause was longer. 'I'm not sure that's a good idea, signorina. He's not expecting you—'

'Please, Sebastiano, I know you don't think me a suitable candidate for Montvelatte's Princess, but if you won't help me get off the island, you have to help me try to make this marriage work. I wouldn't ask if it wasn't important.'

She squeezed the telephone tight in her hand, holding her breath while she waited for Sebastiano's response.

Finally his voice came. 'Can you be ready at nine?'

She breathed out on a grateful sigh. 'I'll be ready.'

Sienna was learning the benefits of having her own staff on hand. A deep oil-scented bath had been drawn for her, plump warmed towels at the ready, a professional hair stylist had miraculously tamed her mass of fiery hair into a sleek updo that shone gold under the lights, and Carmelina had selected and laid out the perfect accessories to the gown she'd decided upon.

She should have felt relaxed after such royal treatment, but inside she felt a tight bundle of nerves that coiled and fizzed and all the while tangled tighter in anticipation. She gave herself a last look in the full-length mirror and smoothed the long satin gloves up her arms, wondering how Rafe would react when he saw her. The sea-green silk gown fitted her almost as snugly as the gloves, the skilful beading around the almost modest bodice-line catching the light like a city lit up at night. Her other gowns had been elegant and perfect princess wear. But tonight she didn't want to play princess. She wanted to play seductress. He'd never seen her dressed in anything like this gown, and she could hardly wait to see his reaction. Then she spun around, glanced over her shoulder, and almost decided he never would.

The backless dress scooped low below her waistline, the beaded border hugging the dress tightly to the curves of her body and shouting *look at me* in the expensive language of designer couture.

She was no catwalk model used to strutting her stuff in make-up and high heels. She was a helicopter pilot more used to wearing overalls and a headset. Was she doing the right thing in trying to get his attention like this, or was she about to make a total fool of herself?

There was a discreet knock at the door. 'Your car is ready, *signorina*,' and the time to change her mind was past.

Carmelina nodded as she handed her the tiny purse that matched her shoes and a gossamer-thin wrap to hang from her elbows. *'Bella,'* she simply said, nodding as Sienna turned for the door.

She descended the sweeping staircase to the ground floor, unable to slow her racing heart or calm her racing mind. Because if this didn't work, if it made no impression on Rafe, and he still failed to see her as the woman she was but for the purpose he was marrying her, then what chance did she have? And what chance their marriage?

The car was waiting, as advised, in the pebbled portico, the duco of the vintage Alfa Romeo gleaming under the lighting. Sebastiano himself emerged to greet her, and for once the smile that greeted her looked more than duty-bound.

'Signorina Wainwright,' he said, with a bow, 'I would be honoured to escort you to Casino de Velatte.'

'You would?'

'It would be my pleasure.'

'Thank you. And I want you to know I'll tell Rafe this was all my idea. I would hate for him to hold you personally responsible.'

'On the contrary,' he said, with a look that was fully appreciative without losing a hint of respect, 'I bow to your wisdom. I think this is a very good idea indeed.'

Either Rafe's secretary seemed incredibly attuned to her state of nervousness, or he was simply good at relating Montvelatte small talk and delivering it in easily digestible chunks as the car wended its way down the mountainside to the city far below.

Whether it was because he thought she needed time to soak in the details, or whether it was because he knew that by saying nothing she would have more time to dwell on—and panic about—the meeting that was to come, she neither knew nor cared. She was just grateful for the company and for the quiet reassurance his presence offered.

Before long the vineyards of the slope had given way to the poplar-lined river road, studded with gated estates and grove after grove of orange trees, and then they were in the city itself, heading towards the harbour on narrow streets squeezed between two- and three-storey buildings, or beside cafés where the patrons spilled out almost to the street.

Sienna gazed out of the window, watching the city and its people, dodging through the scooter-filled traffic, which carried elegant-looking dark-haired women and men with equally dark good looks, and sometimes what looked like entire families hanging on around the driver. There was colour here, life and action, and every trip to Velatte City she found more fascinating.

And then they were on the wide Boulevard Lombardi that separated the hotels and casinos that hugged the shoreline from the marina filled with the latest and greatest in nautical accessories. And there, in the middle of the strip, she could see the dome of their destination glowing green above the surrounding buildings.

'Casino de Velatte is our oldest and most prestigious casino, often referred to as the jewel in Montvelatte's crown,' said Sebastiano from alongside. 'The recital is being held as part of the Casino's bicentennial celebrations.'

The car slowed as they approached, and land that had once been at a premium opened up before them in a series of gardens, each more beautiful than the next with their skilful plantings and water features, and cleverly designed to draw the eye up to where the gardens gave way to the towering forecourt of the grandest casino of them all.

Rafe hadn't brought her here, and she looked at the building in awe. It should be a palace, she decided, as the car pulled up at the doors, the gleaming marble-tiled entrance way glowing gold in warm splashes of light from the crystal chandelier above.

Her door was opened from the outside, and Sienna stepped out into another world, a world featuring not just the opulence of the Castello, but an extravagance she'd never experienced before. Even over the scent of the perfumed garden and the salty tang of fresh sea air, she could almost smell the money.

She didn't belong here.

In a moment of panic she turned back towards the car, but then Sebastiano was at her side, taking her arm, stilling her retreat. He exchanged a few words with the concierge and then was guiding her forwards, through the doors that would lead her to Rafe, and she was never more afraid in her life. She was no seductress. She was no princess. She was a fraud, and there was no way everybody wouldn't know it.

Inside was even more opulent, and the glances they attracted more openly curious, and if it hadn't been for the guiding hand at her elbow, she would have fled in a heartbeat. Instead she was led deeper and deeper into the building, skirting around tables surrounded by the rich and elegant, accompanied by the click and roll of the roulette ball and the hushed murmurs of encouragement to the wheel, past some of the most beautiful women she'd ever seen, wearing figure-hugging gowns, and bearing trays of champagne.

Ushered into a lift adorned in the casino's signature colours of gold, burgundy and navy blue, she let out a long breath.

'You're doing fine,' said Sebastiano, alongside her, reading her like an open book.

She looked over at him, surprised at his encouragement.

'I was wrong about you,' he admitted. 'I was afraid you

weren't what you seemed, that you were wrong for Prince Raphael.'

The lift seemed to have lost all its air. She fanned her face with her hand. 'And now?'

He smiled on a nod. 'I think you will be perfect for him, and for Montvelatte.'

She dragged in a welcome breath. 'Do you think he's going to be angry about me coming here?'

Sebastiano tilted his head a fraction, as if considering his words. Then he smiled. 'I think he's going to be delighted.'

The lift doors opened and they alighted into another opulent lobby, the chandeliers smaller but no less intricate in their workmanship or spectacular in their effect. Twin doors loomed large across the lobby, doors that opened before them, spilling out a group of men talking animatedly.

Sienna stopped as she recognized the man at the helm, and the voices similarly died away as all eyes turned towards her.

At least, she could sense their eyes upon her. Filling her focus front and central was Rafe, resplendent in a dark suit with a burgundy sash that both served to show his tall frame and his broad shoulders to perfection. Sienna felt the primitive sizzle that accompanied Rafe's every appearance, although this time it was tinged with an unfamiliar burst of fear.

So much was at stake.

So much depended on how he reacted to seeing her tonight.

Dry-mouthed she watched his eyes narrow in question, before he came closer, the dark of his eyes warm and rich and assessing every last part of her from her upturned hair to the glint of her satin sandals and every curve along the way. Lingering on those points along the way. Sienna felt her sensitized breasts swell under his scrutiny, her nipples ache as if he'd stroked them with his hot breath. 'Sebastiano,' he acknowledged, without taking his eyes from her, 'what is the meaning of this?'

Sebastiano cleared his throat and murmured his low response, so low that the pack of men behind could not overhear, so low that even Sienna had to strain to catch his response. 'Signorina Wainwright wished to accompany you to the recital.'

Rafe stared at her so hard she took a faltering step back and reached out a hand to Sebastiano for rescue, in case he might suddenly leave without her. 'I'm sorry. It was all my idea. I…I don't have to stay. I can go.'

And then she heard a sound and looked back, and when she saw where he was looking, she realized it had been Rafe who'd made that low guttural noise, Rafe who had spied the gown's clever secret as she'd turned. And the darkness of his eyes gleamed so thick with passion and need that she could feel the heat coming from him, feel it insinuate itself into her flesh and sizzle along her veins.

For the first time, Rafe nodded in Sebastiano's direction. 'Thank you, Sebastiano. You may leave now,' he said, before he slid his hand through her arm and turned to the openly curious audience behind. 'Gentlemen,' he said, with an ease at handling an unexpected situation that she envied, 'Let me introduce to you Signorina Sienna Wainwright, my companion tonight.'

The next few minutes were a blur of names and smiling faces and more hands than she could ever recall shaking in one day. Because it was the scent that coiled inside her now, that marvellous scent of clean unprocessed man. And it was the hand at the centre of her back that had her full attention, the heat generated by the fingers that were stroking her skin and stoking her own need along with it.

Someone pressed a glass of champagne into her hands and she clung to it like a storm-tossed sailor clung to anything he could grasp in the hope of staying afloat. With Rafe filling her thoughts and senses she was in danger of going under.

Finally they were led into a grand ballroom, the dimensions of which took her breath away. What looked like hundreds of people were already seated and waiting for the official party to take their seats—seats, Sienna gathered, that had had to be hastily rearranged in deference to her presence. A hush fell over the crowd as she entered on Rafe's arm and stood beside him in the royal box, a hush that immediately descended into the whispered questioning of a crowd.

Rafe leaned closer to her as the strains of the Montvelattian national anthem died down. 'Do you realise that wearing a dress like that you have well and truly set the cat amongst the pigeons?'

'Do you mind?'

And he gazed down at her with such an intense look of desire that her bones were reduced to jelly. He lifted one gloved hand and pressed the back of it to his mouth. 'What I mind most is that I have to wait until this recital ends before I can take you home and peel that damn dress right off you.'

CHAPTER TEN

SIENNA gasped, the power of his need echoing tenfold inside her, so that right then and there she felt as if he'd already peeled the dress away and that she stood naked and exposed in front of him.

He wanted her. That was good, wasn't it? That was what she had planned. He had to want her if there was any chance it could develop into anything more than a marriage of convenience.

But her plan relied on her being the one in control, the one to steer him to her purpose. Right now, though, she was being carried along on a tidal wave of his making, and that wave was towering and powerful and all-consuming.

And she wasn't sure she wanted the ride to ever end.

The recital had been interminable, the greetings they'd received on their exit taking for ever, and the purposeful silence of the car ride back to the Castello, during which she'd worried that he'd changed his mind, had been an agony.

But finally they were back within the fortified walls, where silence and discretion reigned, and Rafe took her hand and pulled her towards him. 'What did you mean by dressing like that and coming after me tonight?'

She edged backwards, fearful that he'd somehow seen her plan as the desperate attempts of a woman who wanted to be needed, but his arms held her tight and close enough for her to know his intentions hadn't changed in the least. 'Who says I wanted anything?'

His lips curved into a wolfish smile. 'You must want something, to wear a dress designed to make you look like both a virgin and a seductress.'

And she realized he knew nothing, only felt the physical need that she'd hoped he would, the need that was all she had to use to her advantage. 'Which one are you?' he asked her. 'The virgin or the seductress?'

It was easier to play the part she'd assigned herself than she'd ever imagined possible. She let her body lean into his, every curve strategically placed. 'You know I'm no virgin.'

'So what do you want?'

'It's been too long,' she told him, moving her hips just enough that she could feel his rigid length. 'I want you. I want you to make love to me.'

His eyes flared with both victory and red-hot want, and she knew she'd voiced the right words to turn his passion incendiary.

And while that was her own victory, right now the desire to make love with him was the most pressing thing in the world, and that was her obsession.

She didn't have long to wait. His mouth was on hers in an instant, his arms surrounding her, lifting her from the ground and carrying her up the stairs effortlessly, as if she were weightless. Which was exactly how she felt. Weightless. Without a care or a concern or a worry in the world except how to get this man inside her to fill this desperate aching need.

'Christo,' he muttered, as he surged up the stairs, 'but you are driving me insane.'

Once inside his room, he spun her against the closed door, lowering her legs to the ground, clutching the fabric of her skirt so that it bunched in his hands and left her legs near naked. He cupped her behind, his fingers squeezing into her flesh so that she gasped into his mouth. He drank it down, making her gasp once more as his fingers slid under the lace of her thong and worked still lower, while the other hand liberated a breast his hungry mouth soon captured, sucking on one sensitive nipple, tugging at the very essence of her.

Sienna clung to him, her hands tearing at his clothes, pulling his head back to her mouth, wanting to feel more, never satisfied, always wanting more of him in her mouth, on her body—inside—more that she could feel, more of what he gave her with his touch.

He parted her then with his fingers, encountered her slick need, and growled so deep in her mouth that the sound reverberated through her soul. His touch brought flesh already exquisitely tender to flashpoint, and she squirmed against his expert hand, desperation driving her as his fingers toyed with her, teased her, entered her.

She threw her head back against the door, dizzy with it all, and through the wall of his chest she could feel his heart slamming, echoing the crashing beat of her own laboured organ. And still she needed more. Needed him inside her.

As if he read her thoughts, she felt a tug and a snap, heard the hiss of a zip, and felt herself being lifted higher, the heavy door at her back, the liquid silk of her skirt rucked up high on her legs, and the taste of him in her mouth, before he set her slowly down.

Wonder consumed her just as she consumed him, letting him stretch her, fill her, her muscles working to hold him there and never let go. She could stay this way for ever, and it would still not be enough. And then he moved inside her, and the connection sizzled and burned, and before she could fight to hold him, he was gone, balancing on the brink, his breath heavy on her throat as it seemed the world hung in the balance.

And then he thrust inside her again, and this time it was better and deeper than before, the connection more powerful, the union more intense. She clung to him, his every thrust giving her more even as it expanded her need, turning it urgent and desperate and like a living thing.

She felt it rush towards her, unstoppable, inevitable, felt the same juggernaut bearing down on him, heard him meet it head on as he cried out on one final explosive thrust. Powerless to resist, she went after him, her senses exploding until nothing existed but sensation and colour and a world filled with tiny fragments of light.

He recovered first, his breathing still ragged in her ear as he lifted her into his arms again and carried her to the wide bed. He placed her down almost reverentially, kissing her on the forehead, before he turned to remove his jacket and tie and shuck off his shoes.

Sienna blinked back into consciousness and looked up at him, taking in his dark beauty and the stealthy, sexy way he moved, whether with clothes on or off, and felt the first fluttering premonition of trouble.

The sex was good—*great*—and if she'd wanted his complete attention, she had no doubt she now had it. If she was going to make an impression on him, if he was going to see her as a person, a woman with her own needs and wants, if she was going to make him *feel*, now was her chance.

And yet something was wrong.

Deep down inside her, on some fundamental level, something gnawed away at her; something wasn't right.

Rafe turned then, capturing her expression as he unbuttoned his shirt, a small crease appearing between his brows. 'Are you all right?'

'I'm fine,' she lied, her pulse skittering suddenly as her mind tried to get a handle on her unease. She pushed herself up to sitting and wrapped her arms around her knees, feeling ridiculous trying to hold a conversation lying down, while she watched his progress with the buttons down the shirt.

She hadn't meant to watch. Hadn't meant to take any notice. But the way that beautiful sweat-sheened column of olive skin grew longer, as one by one his skilful fingers brought them undone, what choice did she have?

He had beautiful fingers, long and tapered, and what he could do with them…

Oh, my, she rationalized, remembering—who wouldn't feel distinctly shaky when they'd just climaxed in spectacular fashion and a man like Rafe was only now getting around to taking his clothes off?

In preparation for a repeat performance? One could only hope.

He frowned, his face angling to look more closely at hers in the soft light. 'Did I hurt you? Are you feeling unwell? I didn't think to take it slow.'

Distracted by the sudden concern in his voice that brought with it a return of the strange gnawing feeling in her gut, her head got lost between a nod and a shake. 'No. Yes.' She closed her eyes and shook it, this time more decisively. 'Really, you didn't hurt me. I've been fine lately, so long as I avoid certain things.'

And that was the truth. The day she'd arrived at the island, and the following day when she'd tried to leave—those days had been the worst. Since then her morning sickness had been precisely that, a morning phenomenon, and if she was careful, limited to no more than a general queasiness, with no repeat of that early illness. How much of that had been down to stress and the tension of having this man back in her life?

He gave a shrug of his shoulders and peeled the shirt away, letting it drop to the floor, and in the process revealing the full glory of his muscle-sculpted chest, from the wide shoulders and the taut skin to the dusting of hair that focused to a line and drew her eyes down to where it disappeared at his belt. 'I was worried I was too eager for you. I promise this time we'll take it slower.'

She looked up. 'This time.' She repeated the words like a mantra, and he smiled.

'I told you I couldn't wait to remove that dress. I haven't changed my mind.'

Sienna swallowed as he pushed his pants down past hips lean and strong, carelessly stepping out of them. She watched, wide-eyed, as his sleek-fitting black underwear met the same fate, and she stopped breathing altogether when he moved closer. Of course once wouldn't be enough. On their one previous night together, Rafe had shown he had stamina to burn. He knelt on the side of the bed, reached out, and lifted one foot in his hands. Deftly he undid the tiny diamante-studded buckle at the side of her shoe and, holding her ankle in one hand, swept the shoe from her foot with the other, tossing it and the best part of several hundred euros carelessly to the floor behind him.

Vaguely she registered that he must have no idea how much shoes cost, or didn't care, but after a moment, she didn't care either, not when his thumbs started their dance over the ball of her foot. She groaned.

She'd read articles where people had claimed the feet could be erogenous zones, and she'd largely discounted them as fanciful and fictional, but the graze of his fingers, the brush of his skin against the silkiness of her stockings, had her trembling and rethinking her ideas. Or maybe it had nothing to do with her feet and everything to do with the way he looked at her while his fingers worked, dark eyes made darker with desire, more insistent with need.

Or maybe not, she thought, as the other shoe met a similar

fate and Rafe stroked the underside of her foot with his thumbs, causing her back to arch and a sigh of pleasure to erupt from her lips.

'Do you like that?' he said, repeating the action, and she licked her lips and nodded.

'It's…nice.'

'Only nice?' He sounded disappointed. 'Then do you like this?' His fingers trailed up her calf, disappearing beneath a sea of green silk that lapped around her legs like the incoming tide, his fingertips tracing circles higher and higher up her leg.

'It's all good,' she conceded, 'although I can't help but feel a little overdressed.'

He laughed, low in his throat, and the vibrations and the sound were almost enough to bring her undone. He reached up a hand and undid the jewelled clasp at her neck. Instinctively she reached up a hand to prevent the bodice falling down, but he stopped her arm and the fabric slid unrestrained to her waist, releasing her breasts to the air, and to his gaze.

'*Christo,*' he uttered, as he reached for them with his hands, 'but you are beautiful.' His hands cupped her breasts, his thumbs grazing her nipples before he leaned over and took one pink peak into his mouth.

Pleasure speared downwards, like arrows fired and finding their mark, to that place he'd already filled and which ached to be filled again. He worked magic on one breast, and then the other, before lifting his head and swallowing her into the perfect kiss.

She felt his hand low behind her, wondered at his expert discovery of her invisible zip, and felt the cool sweep of air as he tugged down her gown over her hips.

She made a move to remove one satin glove, and he stilled her hands, running his hand along one long satin-cased arm, running another down one silk-clad leg. 'No,' he said, 'leave these. You feel and look exquisite exactly how you are.'

She wanted to believe him, even though her make-up must be smudged beyond repair, her lips pink and swollen, and she could feel her hair coming loose, heavy coiled tendrils even now tumbling around her shoulders. But who was she to argue, when his touch made her feel the seductress she had set out to be?

'You're not angry with me,' she asked on a gasp as he pushed her back into the pillows, his tongue lapping its way first around and then into her belly button, an erotic prequel of what was to follow, 'for coming tonight?'

He lifted his head the merest fraction. 'If I had my way, you would come every night.'

She laughed a husky laugh and shuddered against the bed-clothes, her back arching as his tongue renewed its exploratory journey. 'I meant about coming to the casino. You're not angry?'

His fingers dug into her thighs; his face lay buried in her belly as he grazed her skin with his teeth. 'You have a strange concept of foreplay. What does it take, I wonder, to shut you up.' His teeth nipped at her skin, and she laughed and squirmed again, and he pushed himself higher so his mouth was once again within reach of her nipples. 'But no. Do I look angry?' He paused on the way up, laving at her skin. And he drew one perfect breast deep into his mouth, his tongue circling an even more perfect peak.

She arched into his mouth, her breath quickening. 'It's such a beautiful place.'

'Still won't shut up?' He found her other breast, lavishing the same attention for detail on that one, his hot mouth, his lips and tongue working together like an orchestra.

Teeth grazed her nipple, and she flinched, a deliciously compelling combination of pleasure and pain, a symphony of sensation. 'Sebastiano described it as the jewel in Montvelatte's crown.'

He lifted himself higher, hovering over her as he kissed her eyes, her chin and nose. His lips found hers, teased them open with his tongue and pulled her into a kiss so deep she was lost in it. Then he drew back and she opened her eyes, waiting. Perplexed.

'Sebastiano was wrong,' he said tightly, every angle and plane in his face suddenly accentuated, an exercise in barely restrained control. 'Because *you* are the jewel in Montvelatte's crown.'

And then he plunged into her in one fluid stroke that vanquished the air from her lungs and the conversation from her lips. In that hitched moment, they breathed the same air, shared the same oxygen and, as he filled her completely, shared the exact same space.

Satin-clad hands tangled in his hair, swept the powerful skinscape of his back, and held him to her. Silken-clad legs slid along his, tightening around him and urging him still deeper. And all the while his silken words tangled in her mind, part of the magic, no small part of the sensation.

It might have been a slower build up this time, less frenetic, and with more time to discover and rediscover each other's bodies, but when she came apart, it was a different kind of power that took her shuddering to completion, a different kind of wholeness that brought her back, holding him close, her limbs entwined with his.

A different feeling that left her more confused than ever.

'So that's what it takes to make you shut up.'

Minutes had passed, minutes in which the gradual calming of her breathing belied the growing turmoil of her mind.

Getting him to care for her wasn't supposed to feel like this.

She unburied her face from his shoulder, breathing in his warm male scent, relishing it, even though at the same time the amount she enjoyed it bothered her on another level. 'Apparently.'

Rafe sat up, poured a glass of water from a covered decanter on the bedside table and turned, his eyes brushing along her body as she lay, eyes that took everything in. It was ridiculous to feel shy after what they'd done and what they'd shared, but she still did, still felt exposed. And a trifle ridiculous still wearing stockings and her satin gloves. Then he handed her the glass and she scooted up in the bed, accepting it gratefully, suddenly realising her thirst exceeded her embarrassment.

'I'll speak to Sebastiano,' Rafe continued. 'Get him to free up my diary for a day or two.'

She blinked up at him, hopeful and suspicious in the same motion. 'Why?'

'I've been working too hard. And because we have a lot to catch up on.' He padded across the floor and pulled open a closet, totally at ease with his nudity. And why not, she thought, when you had a body built as if it should be immortalised in marble, every movement revealing the play of superb muscle structure beneath his skin? He was a living sculpture, perfectly proportioned in all the right places, abundantly proportioned where it mattered most. He pulled a white robe from the closet and slipped it over his shoulders, swiping another golden robe from a hanger.

He handed it to her, and for now she clutched it to her chest. 'What did you have in mind?'

'Once news gets out about the wedding, media coverage will make going anywhere a nightmare, but there's still so much you haven't seen here yet. The southern part of the island, for instance. Or we could go for a cruise around the island. Maybe take a closer look at Iseo's Pyramid if you liked?'

'That sounds good,' she heard herself say, not wanting to sound too grateful, too desperate for the opportunity.

He reached out a hand to her and she took it. 'I have to talk to Sebastiano. Why don't you start in the shower and I'll join you shortly.'

She would love a hot shower to massage her spent bones. She'd love it even more with him. She remembered another night, what seemed for ever ago, another promised shower. Maybe this time he might actually join her there. The look in his eyes told him he was definitely planning to.

Her hand in his, she stepped from the bed to the floor. 'So you won't be needing this, after all,' he said, tugging the robe from her hands so it slid to a golden pool at their feet. 'And you won't be needing these any more.' He slowly drew down first one glove and then the other until she was totally naked but for her lace-topped stockings.

His eyes gleamed with heat and fire, his breathing short and hard, and she wondered how it was possible for one man to recover so quickly, and for that man to rekindle the fire in her, so that she too was feeling that familiar ache of need.

He dropped his forehead to hers. *'Dio,'* he muttered, 'what you do to me. But I knew you would come to me.'

'You were so sure?'

'I knew. But had I remembered just how good it could be, I would have taken you that very first night.'

'You tried,' she reminded him, wondering what he'd say or do if he knew the real reason she'd decided to fall back into his bed. 'I didn't let you.'

'It was inevitable,' he said, lifting his head. 'As inevitable as the sun rising in the morning.'

She bristled, having to remind herself what she was trying to achieve and why she even cared. This marriage would happen, she could see no way out, and so she would make of it she damn well could. 'You sound very sure of yourself.'

'I am. As I am sure of you.'

Don't bet on it, she thought, as he let her go to make his call, thinking she knew less and less what it was that she wanted herself.

Don't bet on it.

CHAPTER ELEVEN

WHATEVER Sebastiano had thought of more of his plans being turned upside down, Sienna couldn't imagine, but Rafe had done it, convincing him that another day's meetings could wait. And it was paradise.

Rafe had driven them down the mountain in the sporty Alfa Romeo car, with the top down and the wheels hugging the tight curves as sure-footedly as a cat.

At the marina they'd transferred to the luxury yacht that would take them around the island. It was more like a floating palace, Sienna decided as she was given a tour. Rich mahogany timbers were set off with gold and brass fittings, mirrors and strategic lighting making the most of the space. Not that there was any shortage of that in the vast master suite.

What would it be like to make love in a floating palace, she wondered, looking forward to finding out.

And now up on deck, with Rafe by her side, the launch sliced through the azure water, the wind whipping around them, salt spray sparkling in the air. In loafers and shorts, a casual shirt unbuttoned at his neck and his hair blown freestyle by the wind, he looked magnificent, his olive skin glowing under the sun, his white-teethed smile wide. He looked more relaxed than she'd ever seen him, more together.

He felt even better, his arm looped loosely around her shoulders, his hand on her arm as he pointed out the sights of Montvelatte's coastline, naming the small villages dotted around the cliffs and coves, waving to people in passing vessels, who smiled and cheered when they recognized the royal launch and their new Prince on board.

It was paradise, but it was exhausting, so just as well it was only for a day. The night had been long and full, and the night to come promised to be all of that and more. And Sienna could hardly wait. Even now, just the heat from that looped arm was enough to set her skin to tingling, her pulse to racing. Just the faintest stroke of his fingers against her arm enough to make her nipples ache and firm.

As she'd lain in bed in the dark minutes before dawn, one hand down low on her belly while thinking about the babies growing deep inside and waiting for the first stirrings of the nausea she knew would come, she'd pondered her enthusiasm in his bed, a question that had been plaguing her all day. She'd refused to make love to him when she'd arrived, telling him there was no way she'd sleep with him, fighting off his advances like they were anathema to her. And yet, since the minute she'd invited herself back into his bed, she'd barely been out of it.

But why shouldn't she enjoy making love to him? It merely meant that she enjoyed the sex, the same as he did. It was purely physical. Purely the means to an end.

Sienna looked up at him again, at the chiselled perfection of his jaw and dark beauty of his features, and for a moment was filled with a fear so huge it threatened to consume her. He was a prince, a man whose body and looks would give the gods a run for their money, a man who could move her world with just one heated look, one sensual caress. Why should he ever love her? What could she offer him but to be a willing partner in bed and a mother for his children?

She already represented those things.

Why was she was kidding herself that he would want more? She lowered her eyes, that now familiar gnawing eating away at her gut, leaving a vacuum that she didn't understand and had no way to fill.

'Are you enjoying yourself?'

She turned her face up to his and, even with the sun on her skin, felt the warmth of the smile that greeted her permeate all the way through to her bones. 'Thank you,' she nodded, knowing that whatever happened, she would treasure it forever. 'It's wonderful.'

The boat headed out towards the pinnacle of rock known as Iseo's Pyramid, the mountainous sides reaching further and further into the sky as they approached, the seabirds forming a permanently changing cloud around the peak. Still some distance out, the skipper slowed the engines and cruised gently around the rock; yet even from this distance the rock rose sheer and majestic from the water, its black volcanic walls razor-sharp and magnificent. On one side a tiny beach clung at the base of a cleft in the rock, its white sand framed with wild olive trees and windswept bushes on one side, the jewel-blue sea on the other, and looking like the perfect picnic spot, exclusive, private and with a natural beauty that took her breath away. But there would be no picnic on the beach. 'We can't get any closer,' Rafe explained as the boat bobbed off shore.

And when she looked closer, she could see why, the shadowed outline of rocks submerged just below the surface making any passage through a nightmare, and it was easy to see why the rock had claimed so many victims in its time. For even in the bright light of day, Iseo's Pyramid loomed dark and menacing. To encounter it during a storm would be a living hell.

Sienna leaned against the side of the boat, her eyes scaling the mountain, trying to imagine what it was in the shape of the rock that Iseo had seen on that night, all those years ago.

'Where does the Beast live when it's not in residence, marauding for shipwreck survivors?'

'The Beast of Iseo? It sleeps, far below the sea, busy digesting the contents of another wayward vessel.'

'He must be hungry, then, this Beast of yours, given your embargo on sailings on nights with no moon.'

Rafe turned against the railing and looked down at her, his eyes obscured by dark glasses, yet the hint of a smile tugging at his lips. 'I never thought of that. Do you think it would be wise to make a sacrifice every now and then, in the interests of increasing the opportunities for trade between Montvelatte and our neighbouring countries?'

'Absolutely. Just make sure whoever you sacrifice is a virgin, so I have nothing to fear.'

He laughed, as he had on their cliff walk that evening, and the sound rippled through her on a wave of pleasure, and once again she asked herself why it couldn't be like this always, when one day was so special. He did enjoy being with her. He must feel something for her, to have cancelled his appointments for a day and made the time to be with her. It wasn't all about the sex, or they would never have left his suite this morning.

Shortly afterwards, the launch powered up and steered away from Iseo's Pyramid, back across the passage to Montvelatte. Out on the water the wind was rising. She heard talk from the deck of a predicted summer storm but discounted it. The sky was so blue and cloudless that it reminded her of the years she'd spent with her mother in Australia, where the land had seemed to go for ever until it met the sky. She'd loved the sense of space she'd found there, the space she'd never found growing up on a tiny in-the-middle-of-anocean boat or in a crowded school clinging to the side of a mountain in Gibraltar. Australia had been made of space, it seemed, and Montvelatte, an island in the Mediterranean, seemed to share the best of both her worlds—space and endless skies, hers for the taking.

A wind whipped up, tugging at her hair as the launch sliced through the water. Sienna laughed as she was caught off-balance, the hair flicking loosely around her face, her hands unsuccessfully trying to recapture the wayward locks, until Rafe captured her hands in one of his own and pulled them down low. 'Leave it,' he said, using the sway of the boat to tilt her towards him so he could kiss her brow. 'I love your hair just the way it is.'

And then he angled up her chin, and his lips met hers, her hair blowing unrestrained around them as the empty yawning hole inside her latched onto a single truth that jolted her to her core.

Please, no, she thought, feeling herself shrivel away from him in panic.

Please, not that!

But as his mouth moved over hers, the truth refused to be ignored, unfurling inside her, filling the vacuum in a revelation that could see her damned.

She loved him.

Shock wrenched her from the kiss, and when he came after her she claimed the motion of the boat was making her queasy. He had no trouble believing her, just as she had no trouble convincing him, a wave of nausea snapping closely on the heels of her discovery.

She couldn't love him.

She clung to the railing, while he insisted on fetching her some water, her world tilting and yawing in a way that had nothing to do with the motion of the boat and everything to do with a growing fear in her heart.

How could she have let it happen?

And yet, her mind recalled, one night in Paris, on a night filled with lovemaking so passionate and intense it had rocked her world, hadn't that been exactly what she'd thought? That if a woman wasn't careful, a man like Rafe was everything she could fall in love with?

But that had been before he'd shunted her out the door and out of his life without a second glance, and that was before he'd only wanted her back when he'd discovered she was pregnant to him. How could she fall in love with someone who'd treated her that way?

Too easily, it seemed. She'd allowed the same things she'd been attracted to from the very beginning to influence her now, overriding her reasons to hate him. He'd ridden rough-shod over her at every opportunity, denying her any choice, telling her that they would be married and when. And still she'd let him under her skin, wanted him by her side, in her bed. Wanted him.

And that had been the real reason why she'd wanted to flee from Montvelatte the first chance she'd had. Not just because she was angry with him for the way he'd thrust her from his room that night, but because she'd known, ever since she'd landed on the island, how he could make her feel with just one look or one touch, and so she'd had to escape, and as soon as possible.

And that had been the real reason she'd stayed. Because in spite of everything, he held the magic to make her want him.

And she did want him.

It wasn't supposed to happen this way, though. He could love her, he should love her, but she wasn't supposed to love him, not if he could never return that love.

Sienna clung to the railing, breathing in great bursts of air, as the launch lurched over first one swell, and then another, swallowing them down and wishing she could swallow down her memories. Memories of her mother, her face contorted and tear-stained, her voice cracking as she pleaded with Sienna's father to stay at home and not go to the bar that night. Begging him not to go. Telling him that she loved him.

And her father had bellowed back at her, calling her a stupid bitch, and yelling that he'd never loved her and never would and that the only reason he'd married her was because of the baby she'd been too stupid to get rid of. The hatch door had been slammed shut and he'd gone.

He hadn't come home that night. Or the next. And, worried about her mother's deepening depression, Sienna had asked her where her father was. It had been an innocent enough question. She'd known she was that baby for years, the one who had ruined her father's life. But she'd thought in her young adolescent mind that if she could find her father and tell him that she would leave, things might once again be good between her mother and her father.

She'd only wanted to help.

But her question had only brought fresh floods of tears from her mother that had answered nothing, only bringing on a sick feeling that had buried itself deep into the pit of her stomach—that it was already too late.

And that it was all her fault.

A week later Sienna had overheard the news from her friends at the English school on the side of Gibraltar's mountain, from girls who whispered in the rabbit warren of corridors in hushed tones, that her father had moved in with the woman from the bar and that he'd been boasting to everyone that he was never going back.

In the cramped society that was Gibraltar's marina, it was the best kind of scandal. Sex, infidelity and betrayal, all cele- brated with a tinge of pathos for the child involved, the child who knew she was responsible for it all.

The boat lurched over the wash from a long gone passenger ferry, and a stomach that she'd been trying to keep under control lurched with it. 'Oh, God,' she cried, clamping a hand over her mouth.

Sweat broke out on her forehead; she felt sick to her core and leaned out over the railing, concentrating so hard on not letting go that only vaguely was she aware of the shouting and of the stilling of the boat. She managed a few deep gulps of air, and it was easier then to swallow back on her churning stomach, the residual wash no more than a rhythmic slap of water against the hull.

The gentle breeze cooled her sweated brow, made her aware of how hot she'd been, how close to losing everything in her stomach.

Damn it! She hated feeling this sickness, whatever the cause. Hated the feeling of vulnerability that went along with it.

She felt Rafe's hand at her back, stroking her shoulder, and almost shrugged him away until she realized that if she was feeling anything, then she was already over the worst.

'Here,' he said, and gratefully she turned and took the goblet, sipping at the cool fluid.

'I'll get them to radio the doctor,' he told her. 'He can meet us when we get back.'

She pushed the glass away. 'I don't need a doctor!'

'You're not well. You need a doctor.'

'What I need is to have my head read,' she snapped, wondering what perverse law of nature had decided that, of all the men in the world, she should be unlucky enough to fall in love with this man. 'And I'm quite sure your precious heirs will be fine, which is all you're really worried about.'

His hand fell away, the silence dragging. 'What is this?'

'Just that every time I so much as sneeze, you call in the doctors.'

'I want you to be well. Is there anything wrong with that?'

'You don't give a damn about me and don't pretend you do! Your concern for me extends no further than as an incubator for your babies. If you could get away with plugging me into a power socket for the duration, like any other incubator, you'd be satisfied.'

'You're talking rubbish.' He turned and made a signal to the skipper, who had been waiting patiently for instructions, and who now revved up the engines and cut a course back into port. 'What are you trying to turn this into—some kind of contest about what means more to me? You know how important it is for Montvelatte—for me—to have an heir.'

She swung away from him and swept a hand across her face, pushing back the loose tendrils of her hair. 'There is no contest. I'm merely acknowledging the truth of the matter. You'd never be thinking about marrying me if it weren't for two small smudges on a screen. You'd never even consider marrying me if it weren't for these two babies of yours I'm carrying.'

'And that's a problem?' He moved closer, his hands held out to her, but she jumped back out of his reach just as quickly.

'This damned marriage is all about these babies. Nothing else. If it weren't for them, you would have let me walk away weeks ago.'

His feet planted wide on the deck, he reached a hand to his head, pushing it through his hair, irritation plainly written on his features.

'We've been through this,' he said gruffly, his patience clearly wearing thin. 'We both know why we're getting married. But that doesn't mean we can't be good together. You know that.'

'Sure, we have a great time in bed. Now there's a sound basis for a marriage. Not!'

'Even forgetting the fact we'll have children between us, being compatible in bed is more than some people have.'

'And it's less than others have.'

'I'll settle for the sex.'

She scoffed. 'I'd expect you to say that. And what happens when we don't have such a great time in bed any more? When you get sick of me or I get sick of you? What happens then?'

Even behind his sunglasses, she could see his eyes narrow as they focused in on her. 'Then we get separate beds. Is that what you want to hear?' He looked away, his hand troubling his already tousled hair once more. 'What is this?' he said, turning back. 'What are you trying to prove?'

Sienna stood at the railing, looking out to sea, the wind in her hair as the boat cut through the clear blue water, and shook her head. 'I don't want it,' she said. 'I don't want a marriage based on becoming someone's brood mare.'

'A bit melodramatic, don't you think?'

'No, I don't think. You need an heir. If these...' she placed a hand low over her tummy, cradling the place her babies were growing deep below '...turn out to be girls, that doesn't help you one bit, does it? A daughter cannot become a prince. A daughter does not solve Montvelatte's problem. You need a son.'

'They will be boys; I know it.'

'How can you know it? There is no way of telling at this stage, no way of knowing. And if you're wrong, and neither of these babies is male, what will my job be?' She nodded, drawing herself up as still and tall as she could. 'I'll be expected to keep on breeding until you have an heir and a spare. But will that be enough, I wonder, given what happened to your brothers? Two sons may not be enough. So how many children must I be expected to bear? How many times will I be expected to share your bed so that you might inject me with your seed and get me pregnant? Don't even pretend you don't expect me to be some kind of brood mare for you.'

'Enough!' He drew closer. So close she could see the

corded tension in his throat, the thump of his heart beating in his temples. 'And you would have me believe that you do not enjoy sharing my bed? *Dio*, who was it who dressed herself like a temptress and paraded herself in front of Montvelatte's wealthiest like some high-society whore, trawling for sex, smelling for all the world like a bitch in heat—'

Her open palm collided against his face with a crack that slammed his head sideways and left a deep red stain upon his olive-skinned cheek.

'You bastard! I am *nobody's* whore!'

He raised a hand to his face, rubbing the place she had hit and all the while he looked down at her. 'All I am trying to do is make the best of a situation.'

'Take advantage of it, you mean!'

'Which is better than pretending it doesn't exist! Don't you think it's about time you faced the facts? You're pregnant with twins. *My* twins. What the hell else are you going to do?'

'I don't know. But maybe you might have bloody well asked me to marry you, instead of just demanding I do.'

'And would you have said yes?'

'Not a snowball's chance in hell.'

His jaw worked overtime, his eyes cold as flint. 'Then maybe it's just as well I didn't ask.'

CHAPTER TWELVE

THE engines slowed as they entered the harbour, and Rafe went and stood at the opposite side of the launch as the pilot skilfully negotiated their way into the marina and to the private landing where Sebastiano stood to attention, waiting for them to dock, the buttons on his jacket gleaming under the sun. He was looking from one to the other, a small frown creasing the skin between his wiry eyebrows.

'What is it?' Rafe asked before they'd berthed, obviously eager for a change of topic.

'The Princess Marietta has arrived. She's waiting for you at the Castello.'

'Marietta is here? Already?' He leapt onto the dock. 'I'll take the Alfa. Sebastiano, you take Signorina Wainwright and drive carefully. She's feeling a little off-colour.'

And then he was gone, and it was Sebastiano's duty to hand her from the boat. 'You're not well, Signorina Wainwright?' he inquired as intelligent eyes scanned her features, and she gained the distinct impression he missed nothing, not even the residual spark of fury that coloured her vision.

'I'm fine,' she answered, taking his hand as she stepped onto the dock. 'Rafe worries too much.'

'Prince Raphael has not seen his sister in some years. They have a lot to catch up on.'

'Lucky Marietta,' was the best response she could dredge up.

* * *

He'd tried. He'd cancelled his appointments and taken her out on a cruise around the island. He'd shown her the tiny coves and beaches that dotted the coastline, tutored her in the names of the villages and what specialities each was renowned for, whether it was to do with wine, olives, oranges or seafood.

Rafe took a hairpin bend, his tyres squealing in protest, and slammed his fist against the steering wheel. He'd done everything he could. And still she railed against him, blaming him, fighting the inevitable as if she were some innocent lamb being led to the slaughter.

Christo! What was her problem?

Last night she'd been the one to come to him, calling to every last sexual sense he had, the siren, beckoning him, wanting him to make love to her.

Hadn't he given her what she'd wanted? She'd seemed fine with their arrangement then. What the hell had changed between then and now?

The Alfa Romeo made easy work of the climb, the Castello looming larger and larger in front of him as he neared its iron gates. Maybe she was right. Maybe their marriage was a disaster waiting to happen if she could run so hot and cold in the space of twenty-four hours.

Maybe he would be better off with someone more amenable. Or maybe pregnancy was sending her hormone levels haywire. She was having twins after all. Did that mean twice the hormones?

Besides, he didn't want someone else.

Why would he when she was already pregnant with his seed?

Two babies. And she could think what she liked, but he was damned sure at least one of them would be a son and the heir that Montvelatte needed if it was to maintain its status as a Principality into the future.

It was perfect. Why couldn't she see that?

It had to be hormones.

Rafe pulled into the forecourt and was just uncurling himself from the car when he heard a sound, a familiar voice even as it turned into a squeal of pleasure. He looked up to see his little sister running down the steps towards him, and he wondered when his little sister had turned into such a stunning woman, a younger version of how he remembered his mother—blonde and beautiful and a throwback to another time, when northern Europeans had swept south into Italy. Somehow Marietta had inherited the lion's share of her genes from their mother. As for him, he'd inherited her height, but the rest of his genes he could attribute squarely to his typically Mediterranean father.

He was glad she'd won their mother's blonde good looks and that they sat with such apparent ease on her. Maybe he hadn't taken any notice back then, or maybe it had just been too long a time since he'd seen her. How many years was it since they'd seen each other? Whatever, it was way too long.

'Raphael!' she squealed, launching herself at him, and the years faded away, and it was his little Marietta back in his arms. His same little princess. Although now with a discernible hint of a New Zealand accent. 'I'm so sorry I missed your coronation.'

He grimaced. 'Don't be. It was a dry and dusty affair. You didn't miss anything. But you're here early. I wasn't expecting you until just before the wedding.'

'I finished a design project early. Thought I'd take off before they lumbered me with another. I hope you don't mind. It's just so good to see you at last.' She kissed both his cheeks and then stood back down, a grin tugging at her lips as she gave him a look of mock seriousness. 'Or should I call you "Prince Raphael" now?'

He squeezed her to him again and spun her around, returning the kiss with one of his own. 'Only if you let me call you princess.'

'But you always did,' she said on a laugh as she settled back to ground level, taking his arm as they headed into the Castello. 'But who would have imagined one day I would actually be a princess for real—and that this—' she swept her arm around in a wide arc '—would all be yours.'

'It's not mine. Technically, I'm just looking after it.' She turned and switched on that same electrifying smile that had got his mother noticed by a prince who'd lost his wife, only to be thrust into oblivion when he had tired of her, and something tugged at him from way deep inside.

This hadn't been a happy place for his mother, bearing babies who were destined never to rule, in love with a man who had only sought her comfort on the rebound.

'You always were a stickler for doing it by the book,' she said with another laugh, dragging him away from the pit where lay his memories of the time. 'Can't you sit back and enjoy it, just a little? I've been having a ball looking around this old place. I only know it from photographs.'

He led her into the library, the aroma of fresh coffee and warm rolls reminding him that he'd had a full appetite-building day on the water, a day that had ended less than spectacularly, which meant the comfort factor of the food wasn't lost on him either. He sat down and poured coffee for them both, adding a liberal dash of cream to his own.

Marietta took the cup he proffered, slipped off her shoes, and curled them beneath her, holding her cup with both hands as she blew across its surface. 'Plus I think I have incorporated into my memories all those things I heard you and Mama talking about—when you did talk about Montvelatte.' She took a sip of her coffee, and when she spoke again her voice

was subdued. 'I can't believe what happened to our father. He
never cared for us, never gave us a thought, but I thought he
loved his sons. How they could do such a thing to their own
father—' She looked up at him. 'Have you seen them at all,
Carlo and Roberto?'

Rafe leant back in his chair and stretched his legs out long
in front of him. 'I visited them once in the prison.'

'And?'

He remembered the day, before his coronation, when he'd
gone to see them. He wasn't even entirely sure why he'd
wanted to go, just that if they could talk, maybe he could make
some sense of what had happened, but all he'd got was their
hatred, their sneers and looks of derision, reminding him how
he had felt long ago, as if he was still the bastard son who
counted for nothing. He shook his head. 'Nothing's changed.'

She blinked and took a deep breath, then turned her eyes
up at him over the cup and smiled apologetically. 'What am
I talking about? You're getting married, big brother. How
amazing is that?'

'Why should it be amazing? I'm thirty-three years old.
High time I settled down, wouldn't you say?'

She laughed and put her cup down. 'Except you were the
one who was never going to settle down.'

He looked away. Wondered why he hadn't yet heard any
sound of Sebastiano returning with Sienna.

'Where is she?'

'What?'

'Your fiancée. Where is she? When do I get the chance
to meet her?'

'Oh.' He shook his head. 'Soon. I'd like you to be one of
her bridesmaids. It's probably just as well you're here early.'

'That's what I figured,' she said, sipping at her tea inno-
cently. 'Anyone else I know in the wedding party?'

'Probably only Yannis. I've asked him to be my best man, of course.'

The cup stilled at her lips, and something briefly clouded her eyes, something he didn't quite understand, before she looked up at him and threw him one of those dazzling smiles that lit up the room. 'Of course. Who else? Anyway, what's she like, this bride of yours. Tell me about her. This is so amazing, big brother, I've never know you to stick with a woman for more than a month in your life. She must be something to have got you to commit.'

'She is,' he said with surprise, his voice choking, his ears straining for any sound. 'You'll meet her soon.'

'Is she pretty?'

He jerked his head around, his fingers tangling together, his feet itchy, unable to keep still. Was she pretty? In his mind's eye he saw her hair, coiling around her face, refusing to be restrained, and shining copper against the most perfect translucent skin. *Dio*, she wasn't just pretty, she was breathtaking, a breath of fresh air on a stifling summer's day, a slice of paradise in every smile. 'She'll make a great first lady for Montvelatte,' he said, realising how lame the words sounded the minute they'd left his mouth.

Marietta considered him carefully, her long-lashed eyes as calculating as any computer. 'But you love her, right?'

Sienna had made a hash of the afternoon. Blown any sense of camaraderie she and Rafe had been building up because she'd had an epiphany. An epiphany she wanted to run kicking and screaming from. A thunderclap that, at first, had seen continuing her endeavours to make him love her all but pointless.

She'd wanted to wallow in the depths then. She deserved to wallow. To consider herself lost, like some storm-tossed traveller at sea, miles from home, without a sign of land, and bereft of loved ones. Iseo's Pyramid had never looked so appealing.

But there was no escape, and nothing would change the truth. She loved Rafe Lombardi. *Prince Raphael Lombardi.* She wasn't supposed to love him, but she did.

And she could deny it all she wanted. She could rail against the injustice of it. She could drive herself and everyone around her crazy by fighting it and fighting them, but then what good would that do?

Or she could keep going with her plan. Just because her father had never loved her mother, didn't mean that Rafe could never love her. She was sure he felt something for her. There was a spark—something—that was worth pursuing, no matter how much he tried to compartmentalize her usefulness in his life between recreation and procreation.

It was no consolation that her mother had probably felt just as sure that she would be able to make Sienna's father love her. It was no help at all.

But if she was to win through this, then she had to look to the positives. Rafe could love her, she was sure.

She had to be sure.

Sebastiano seemed to respect her need for quiet and drove at a gentle pace up the mountain to the Castello, the shadow thrown by the building casting the road into a half-light that seemed strangely to fit her mood.

Half-light. Where she felt now, knowing she loved Rafe. Knowing he didn't love her.

Half-light. A possible future of unreciprocated one-way affection if she didn't try.

Did she want to live life that way? Hell, no.

Rafe's car was still in the driveway when they pulled up, but something else captured her attention. The JetRanger sitting pretty in the centre of the helipad below, the familiar navy-and-white colours of her former employer proudly displayed. Just the sight of it was enough to rip open the scar of losing her recent life.

Sebastiano opened the door for her, caught the direction of her lingering gaze, and sought to explain. 'Princess Marietta arrived in it two hours ago. I believe the pilot is waiting to collect a delivery before taking off.'

She turned to him. 'Who's the pilot? Do you know?' She hadn't been with the company that long, but just the thought of connecting with someone from her former life—anyone— lifted her spirits immeasurably.

Sebastiano gave a nod. 'I will find out for you. But if you would like to step inside, I dare say Princess Marietta would like to meet you.'

Sienna hesitated a fraction longer, her gaze on the chopper, her fingers itching to hold a joystick again. She'd missed flying, missed being part of the endless sky. A gust of wind came from nowhere, and her eyes scanned further afield, to where the sky was deepening and even the water below was chopping up, looking more threatening. Maybe they were right. A summer storm. That would be something to see.

Then, with one last look at the helicopter, Sienna followed Sebastiano inside.

She heard voices coming from the library, Rafe's rumbling deep tones and a woman's voice, her laughter light and infectious, and, without having even met the woman, Sienna liked her already. It would be nice to have another woman around, nice to have someone to talk to, and she was about to enter the room when she heard it.

'But you love her, right?'

Sienna stopped short of the doorway, holding her breath, her senses on red alert. There was only one person they could be talking about.

The silence stretched on for ever as Sienna waited, her ears straining to hear his response over the pounding of her heart.

'Did you know she was pregnant?'

She looked to the ceiling, her fingers clenching and un-clenching as Rafe deftly sidestepped the issue. From inside the room, she heard the sounds of Marietta's delight, her squeal when she heard the news about the twins, while outside the room Sienna closed her eyes and breathed deep. She knew she couldn't keep standing here eavesdropping forever. She would have to enter the room, meet Rafe's sister, and pretend everything was all right. When nothing was right and every-thing was all wrong.

Desperately wrong, when a perfect day could turn upside down. Where a fragile peace was going to be the best they could ever hope for.

She couldn't meet Marietta now, couldn't pretend that ev-erything was all right and that she was the blushing bride. Brides were supposed to look radiant, and right now she didn't have a sailor's chance against Iseo's Pyramid of pulling that off. As quietly as she had come, she turned and headed for the stairs.

'So, big brother,' his sister said, 'anyone would think you were avoiding the question. You do love her, then?'

His sister hadn't changed a bit. He'd thought he'd thrown her off topic with the news of the twins, but she could always be like a dog with a bone when it suited her. He got up and walked to the windows, noticed the darkening sky and the brooding light, but it was on noticing the car parked next to his that he frowned. *Where was she?* He turned back to his sister. 'You always were a hopeless romantic, Marietta.'

'And you were always a hard-nosed cynic.'

'With good reason!'

She got up and joined him at the window, her hand on his arm. 'Raphael, what happened to Mama, it doesn't have to be like that.'

'It won't be. I've made sure of it. Sienna will make the perfect wife.' *Once she could get her hormones under control.*

'Without love?'

'We get on fine.' *Although, given today's events, it could be better.*

'So,' she continued, and he sighed, knowing the interrogation was far from over, wishing Sienna would arrive so that he might be spared, and his sister would turn her powers of inquisition in her direction. 'You're marrying this woman, who's carrying your twin babies and who is expected to become part of some royal fishbowl, but you don't love her?'

'It's easier that way,' he said, turning his attention once more out the window, Iseo's Pyramid growing more evil-looking in the darkening sky, the usual cloud of seabirds absent, as if they'd all already hunkered down for the storm.

'So what's in it for her?'

'She gets to be a princess. Isn't that every little girl's dream? It used to be yours.'

Marietta conceded his point with a nod. 'Although my father was a prince, so it's slightly different. But is Sienna happy with that?'

'She will be.'

'And she doesn't love you?'

'Of course not!' And after the things he'd said to her today, he'd be surprised if she was even talking to him. He flinched when he remembered. He shouldn't have likened her to a high-class whore. She hadn't deserved that.

'Just as well.'

'What do you mean?'

'Only this, big brother. Our mother adored our father and

all for nothing because he was incapable of returning that love. She died lonely and bitter because of it. So if you care at all for this woman, don't let that happen to her.'

He had to prise his teeth apart in order to speak. 'It won't.'

Rafe found her in her room, collecting up her damp towels, freshly showered and smelling like a new morning after a night of rain showers. And even in the jeans and singlet top she'd changed into, her hair pulled into a loose ponytail behind her head, she looked so beautiful that the desire to possess her swelled up large in his chest.

'Marietta was hoping to meet you.'

Her eyes were cool, noncommittal, and he figured she was still angry with him from their argument on the boat. 'I'm sorry. I needed to freshen up. Is she staying?'

He nodded, watching her carefully, searching for any sign that Marietta could be right, and that Sienna might somehow have fallen in love with him. 'She's joining us for dinner.'

'Fine.' She made a move towards the bathroom with the wet towels.

'Sienna…'

'What?'

'Somebody else will get those.'

'They're only towels. It's no trouble to hang them up.'

He followed her into the bathroom. 'Look, I shouldn't have said what I did, on the boat.'

She looped one towel over the rail, not even looking at him. 'Which bit, exactly?'

He reached a hand behind his neck and massaged muscles tight and stiff. 'When I likened you to some high-society whore. I shouldn't have said that.'

She sniffed, sliding the other towel over the rail to join the first, fussing with the edges so they exactly aligned. 'I don't know, I actually thought referring to me as "some bitch in heat" was equally as offensive.' Satisfied with the placement of the towels, she turned and pushed past him, back into the bedroom, sitting down on the bed, slipping sandals on her feet.

'I was angry.'

'I'll say, not that I think that excuses you. Seems to me that it's okay for you to demand sex and to tell me that you want me, but that the moment I do, I'm some kind of whore.' She stood up. 'How does that double standard work, exactly?'

'I'm sorry. I was out of line.'

'Yes, you were. Now, if you'll excuse me?'

'Where are you going?'

'Just for a walk.' She felt no compunction to tell him where and what for, no need to tell him that the pilot of the helicopter was a former colleague and that she was looking forward to talking to someone she'd known longer than ten minutes. Sebastiano had promised her he'd be able to give her a few minutes before the chopper had to take off, before the curfew came into effect. 'To clear my head.'

'The wind's getting up. Don't take the cliff walk.'

This time she managed to dredge up a smile. 'No. I wouldn't dream of it.'

'And, Sienna.'

She turned just inside the door. 'Yes?'

'Marietta was worried about you.' He noticed the slight frown that puckered her brow. 'I thought I should say something.'

Her frown deepened. 'About what?'

'About how things are between us. About how they have to be.'

He had her full interest now, every cell in her body sitting up and taking notice. She shut the door and turned towards him, crossing her arms in front of her. 'So tell me.'

'This won't be a normal marriage.'

She gave a brief laugh. 'You think I haven't picked up on that? But why should Marietta be worried about me. We've never even met.'

'Because of what happened to my mother. A long time ago.' He dragged in a breath and threw his eyes to the ceiling, looking as if he'd rather be anywhere but here, and meanwhile she waited, caught between wanting to flee and to protect her emotions from yet another roller coaster ride, and wanting to stay and hear what he had to say. To get to the bottom of his fears and hang-ups, to have him open up to her about his family and what made him the person he was—surely he wouldn't do this unless she meant something to him? She didn't want to raise her hopes, only to have them cut down again. But neither could she live without hope. Had Marietta made him see something he hadn't seen himself?

'My father's first wife died suddenly,' he began, 'and he was left to raise two young sons.'

'Carlo and Roberto,' she said quietly, filling in the blanks, and he nodded.

'He was devastated for a time, thrown completely by her loss and by the unexpected responsibility of deciding what happened to the next generation. My mother was enlisted to help the nanny, and she was very beautiful. When you meet Marietta you will see what I mean; she is very much like her mother, who was not only beautiful, but a rare blonde in an island filled with dark-haired people. She stood out and she was noticed. My father was still grieving his lost wife, but he was smitten with my mother's beauty and seduced her, wanting no more than relief from the anguish of losing his wife. Meanwhile she was young and overcome by his apparent affection, and she had fallen in love with him.

'When she became pregnant, he moved her out of the palace, but still he went to her. And still my mother took him in. I think she believed that one day he would marry her and make her his princess.

'But she fell pregnant again. Meanwhile my father found another mistress, younger and with more time on her hands, and my mother was distraught. He sent her away, offering her a settlement if only she never returned. So she left.'

The seconds ticked away, an antique mantel clock that she never noticed except for the deepest, darkest nights, sounding like a drumbeat in the ensuing silence, with only the wind whistling outside for company.

'Why are you telling me this?'

'So that you know the risks.'

'Risks?' She battled to make sense of it all. 'I still don't understand. What's your mother got to do with me?'

His eyes were so dark and deep, she felt in that moment she could fall into them and never find her way out. 'She fell in love with a man who was incapable of loving her. I'm warning you not to do the same thing.'

CHAPTER THIRTEEN

THE wind suddenly howled outside the windows, a loose shutter somewhere banging. But inside the room, Sienna's blood had turned to ice, her heart stilled with the cold.

'You're warning me off.'

Rafe nodded.

'Telling me not to fall in love with you?'

'Telling you how it has to be.'

'Because you don't love me.'

'Because I can't love you. I can't love anyone.'

She shook her head, the injustice of it all threatening to swamp her, the sheer unfairness too much to comprehend. 'But you don't know that.'

'I know what I saw what my mother go through. I know I will never put myself in such a position.'

'And you're trying to tell me that this is the only way this marriage can work, by you not loving me and me not loving you.'

He held up his hands. 'We can still have a good marriage.'

She took a step back towards the door, the pleas of her mother running through her head, begging her father not to leave them. The sound of her father yelling back, telling her that he'd never wanted her, that he'd never loved her. The sound of the hatch slamming down, as he'd left them for ever.

That was not going to be her future. But it would be if she married Rafe. She could fight and fight and do everything she could to try to make him love her, but his mind was made up. She'd already lost him.

'No.'

His eyes narrowed, his stance more alert. 'What do you mean, *no*?' And just like his stance, the tone of his voice had also changed, shifting from conciliatory to wary in a moment when he realized he didn't have the upper hand any more.

'I'm not prepared to marry you on those terms. I could never marry someone who didn't love me—who was incapable of loving me. Don't you see? My mother was just the same as yours. She loved my father with all her heart, and he turned that power back on her and crushed her with it. And nothing, not even the child that had forced them into marriage, was enough to keep them together.

'I made a promise to myself years ago that I would never marry a man for the sake of an unplanned pregnancy, especially without that man's love.' She looked at him, her eyes scanning his features, wanting to imprint his face on her memory so that she might remember every last perfect detail of him in case it was the last time she saw him this close, beginning to believe it might very well be. 'And I was starting to think it might work. I thought there was a chance—that we could make it work. But, no. I can see that's not possible.' She glanced at her watch, cursing to herself when she saw the time. So much for catching up with an old colleague. The chopper was probably already gone, just one more disappointment in what had turned out to be a gut-slammer of a day. But that didn't matter right now. She just wanted to get away, find some space, sort out a head too full of cries of injustice and a heart too shredded with pain.

She reached for the door, pulling it open. 'I guess the only bright spot is that it's lucky we had this conversation now, before we went through that farce of a marriage.'

The door slammed shut, Rafe's hand and his weight behind it. 'What the hell are you saying?'

She stared up at him, surprised he'd moved so fast. Unsurprised at his anger. He'd still expect her to marry him come hell or high water. What did it take to make him realize nothing could make her settle for a loveless marriage? 'What do you expect? You don't leave me with much choice. I can't marry you, Rafe, babies or no. I can't stay here with a man who can't love. I won't be my mother all over again.'

'Who's asking you to? You said yourself that your mother loved your father. It doesn't have to be that way for us. That's what I'm trying to prevent.'

She laughed then, a release so unexpected that it left her almost dizzy in its wake, dizzy and so close to tears she could feel the moisture seeping through. 'But that's the problem, Rafe, it's already too late. Because I…I love you.'

Stunned didn't come close to expressing the way Rafe felt. She couldn't be serious. She couldn't be.

Dio! He wheeled around, both hands clutching at his temples, tangling into his hair, searching for answers he couldn't find. It was the last thing he wanted to happen. It was the worst thing that could have happened.

'I don't believe you.'

I don't want to believe you.

'You think right now I care what you believe?'

'Yet you say you love me.'

'Do you think I want to? Do you think I went looking for love with a man who practically dragged me kicking and screaming into a marriage I didn't and still don't want? What kind of masochist do you think I am?'

He couldn't answer. He didn't know. All he knew was that

something was wrong, his convenient marriage slipping beyond reach, sliding towards a disaster he'd never seen coming.

A disaster he'd been trying to avoid ever since he'd been a child.

'Don't waste your time on love.
Don't lose your heart.'

He couldn't love and, damn it all, she wasn't supposed to love him.

He looked up at her, at her face of porcelain-like skin, at her hair kissed gold by the sun, her eyes wide with questions he knew he'd never be the one to answer. And inexplicably he ached with that knowledge, the gears in his chest crunching and grinding together.

And he didn't have the faintest idea of how to stop them.

'You must go,' he said, his voice a coarse whisper, while in his mind the tear-streaked face of his mother played, kissing him goodnight the nights she'd managed to stay up longer than he did, the scent of perfume more and more giving way to the fumes of alcoholic despair. He didn't want that fate for Sienna, but neither could he bear to witness it here, where he couldn't give her what she needed. 'Get out now, before it's too late!'

She hovered uncertainly, her eyes shining, or was that merely his?

'Rafe,' she said, putting out a hand to him. 'It doesn't have to be like this. Can't we talk about it? There must be a way, has to be a way.'

'There is no way!'

'But your babies. One day we will share children, maybe even the heirs Montvelatte needs. You're not thinking straight.'

'Send me the first-born son!' he yelled, the pulse in his head pounding like drums. 'You can keep the other.'

She reeled back as if he'd physically thrust her aside. 'Rafe. I'm sorry.'

'No, you're not! You've been trying to figure out a way to get out of this marriage from day one. And now you've finally hit on the perfect plan. You knew I could never do to a woman what my father had done to my mother. I'd told you what he'd done! What better way to secure your release.'

'Rafe, it's not like that. Listen to me. I love you.'

'And for the last time, I don't want your love! Get out. Go! I never want to see you again.'

Blinded by tears she could no longer control, Sienna somehow stumbled out of the room, blundering past curious staff, who called out to her in concerned voices, past the palace guard that had held her hostage that first day and now stood by to let her flee.

Outside the wind tugged at her hair, the sky an ominous shade of grey, but she took no notice, running full pelt for the one person she knew might help her. The one place where escape lay waiting.

It was still there, the small pick-up truck just driving off. Any minute the JetRanger and her lifeline to the outside world would be gone. She screamed out, but her words were carried away on the wind, and the pilot climbed into the cabin and pulled his door shut.

She had time. She knew the time he would take to get the bird off the ground, to turn on the master electrical switch and avionics, to check fuel levels and turn the fuel valve master on.

She was halfway down the road as the navigation lights turned on. Right on cue.

She pushed herself harder as the rotors began to turn, ducking down low as she made for the pilot's door, her fist slamming on the window.

The pilot, Randall, looked around, first in shock, a smile of recognition tinged with concern spreading his lips wide a moment later before he opened the door. 'Hey, there,' he said in his lazy American drawl. 'I thought you weren't coming. What's up?'

She gulped down air into burning lungs and did her best to smile while she swiped away at her damp cheeks. 'No time for small talk. Just get me out of here.'

'I love it when a lady tells me exactly what to do.' He grinned and waited until she was in the seat alongside him, her seatbelt buckled, before he raised the helicopter from the ground. 'You almost missed me,' he said, shouting to make himself heard. 'Any later and we would have been stuck here for the night. Damn curfew.'

She nodded, still trying to regain her breath. She knew all about the damn curfew.

'We missed you at the office,' Randall said, as the bird moved under his expert hands. 'Been taking a vacation?'

'You could say that.'

He flicked a glance into the back. 'You didn't bring any luggage.'

'Sudden change of plans.'

'Only there was this rumour going 'round, y'know, that you were maybe stuck on Montvelatte for good.'

'Big storm coming,' she said, pointing out the windscreen, and the pilot beside her laughed. 'I get the picture. And, yeah, it might get a bit bumpy, so hang on.'

The bumps didn't worry her, at least not the bumps in the air. It was the bumps that life dealt out that were infinitely worse. She turned around, trying to gauge their distance from the island, wondering when she'd ever be far enough. Escape had been ridiculously easy in the end. But, then, Rafe had practically thrown her out.

Sienna sat back down in her seat, letting out a long breath. To their left the looming peak that was Iseo's Pyramid claimed sovereignty over the surrounding waters, a dark prince in a darker sea, and she shivered as she let her gaze drift over its frightening dimensions, its sheer size just as overwhelming from above as below. She wasn't afraid. She'd left the real Beast of Iseo behind on Montvelatte, but still the dark brooding shape held the power to fascinate, the power to disturb.

She sensed it rather than heard it, something no passenger would notice but an experienced pilot would. She looked across at the pilot and then down at the gauges at the exact same time he did. 'What is it?'

'I don't know.' His eyes scanned the controls, nothing evident, and then it happened again, a tiny blip, a momentary loss of power, and this time Randall's hands were hard at work. 'Damn,' he yelled. 'Whatever it is, we'll have to turn around back to Montvelatte.' And her spirits plummeted. To be foiled when she was so close to escape! How could she return to that island? How could she ever risk facing him again, the man who had banished her because she had been foolish enough to love him? But right now there was no other choice.

Then a bolt of lightning rent the sky in two, the world around her appearing in black and white, like some crazy negative, and she would have sworn the bolt hit the very rock itself. Birds erupted from the peak like magma from a volcano, a cloud of huge seabirds, panicked from sleep and lumbering through the air in every direction. Normally they would have been fine where they were, far enough from the rock and the wheeling cloud of birds that they would be in no danger, but these birds were stunned, beyond instinct other than to escape.

'Watch out,' she cried, as Randall continued to do battle with the handicapped craft. But it was already too late. There was a bang as something hit the rotors and the aircraft shuddered and yawed to one side, the smell of smoke filling the cockpit. And now she was helping him with the controls, battling to put the chopper into autorotation and regain control, but it was no use.

'We're going down,' he called, 'we won't make it to the island.' But she was already at the radio, barking out a Mayday call.

'Head for the rock,' she said, and the pilot tossed her a look that said she was as mad as Iseo himself. 'There's a small beach,' she shouted, clutching at the controls, 'around the side.' And the only place they had a chance of making an emergency landing.

For a few hairy seconds she almost thought they would make it, the two of them almost enough to get the helicopter under control. Until the second bird hit. It penetrated the cockpit like a missile, a sickening crunch that sprayed blood and gore everywhere as it slammed into the pilot.

'Randall!' she screamed, as he slumped over his controls, feathers stuck to blood she had no way of knowing belonged to him or the bird.

She battled to push him back into his seat while trying to manage the controls for both of them, the rock looming ever larger, the wind wilder where the rock ended and the sea began.

And then there it was, the tiny patch of sand, barely visible in the growing darkness but there, calling out to her like an invitation, a siren's call.

'Let's hope not,' she muttered through grim lips as she battled the wind and rock and a failing aircraft.

Rafe was still fuming, stalking around Sienna's room, waiting for her return, when Sebastiano found him. 'Prince Raphael,' he said with a small bow.

'Not now,' he said gruffly, turning away, not interested in the minutiae of the affairs of state when something of momentous proportions had just taken place. Something he was still battling to get a handle on.

Sienna had said she loved him. Why? How could it have happened when their mothers' stories were so similar? How could she embrace love after what her mother had gone through?

But she *hadn't* embraced it.

He thought about her arguments, her protests. She hadn't wanted to love him. Something he could identify with.

And yet she did love him. There was something totally un-identifiable about that. Though, at the same time, something unexpectedly and oddly satisfying.

'I think you will want to hear this.'

'Didn't you hear me? I said, not now!' He was still trying to make sense of it, trying to work out why his gut felt so twisted and torn and just plain wrong when he'd done what he'd thought was right and got rid of any chance of someone loving him.

Except knowing he'd achieved that didn't make him feel any better. It made him feel a damn sight worse. And he was damned sure his father had never felt this bad when he'd exiled his mother, or he would have changed his mind in a heartbeat and kept her for his own.

And the gears crunched some more before settling into a new configuration, something that worked on a different level.

And he remembered another time, another evening, when he'd walked that cliff-top walk with her, and he'd felt the swelling inside that had told him that this marriage would work, and at last he realized what that feeling had truly been. Not a beast inside him, needing to be fed, but a heart so crusted in tragedy and pain that it had taken a woman like Sienna to shed light and crack it free.

He hadn't had to make her see this marriage would work. She'd shown him the light, she'd made it possible.

He couldn't send her away, because he needed her here now, with him every day of his life. And without fully understanding why, something told him that he had missed an opportunity back there in her room to tell her what he really thought, feelings he was still trying to come to terms with, feelings that would not be suppressed, no matter how much he denied them.

'But it concerns Signorina Wainwright.'

The wind gusted around the castle then, pummelling the walls and rattling windows until they shook, and a niggling seed of premonition buried itself inside him and took root.

'What is it?'

'She was seen leaving in the helicopter. The one that brought Princess Marietta.'

He looked to the windows, where the tops of trees could be seen dancing wildly in the wind, leaves flying past, the rumble of thunder like an omen.

'She's out in this? Why the hell didn't anyone stop her?'

Sebastiano crossed his hands in front of him and dipped his head. 'That's not all. There's been a Mayday call reported from the helicopter. Some kind of electrical fault, coupled with a birdstrike.'

Rafe didn't hear the words. He felt them like boulders raining down, their pain etching his soul. 'How far did they get from the island?'

'The *Guardia Costiera* has been alerted, although in these conditions...'

'How far did they get?'

Sebastiano hesitated, clearly uncomfortable with imparting his next piece of information.

'Iseo's Pyramid.'

Rafe's blood ran cold. He'd sent her away. He'd told her to go. He might as well have sent her to the very Beast himself. *Christo*, why had it taken so long for him to realize what should have been so obvious all along? That he wanted this woman because he loved her, in spite of every warning he'd had, he loved her.

And he wanted her back.

Ice filling his veins, he somehow made it to the rain-lashed terrace, his eyes searching out the familiar black outline of rock against the clouds and the storm tossed sea. But there was no missing it. Not today, even on the darkest night, no missing that other cloud that rose unnaturally from the other side of the island.

A single plume of smoke.

CHAPTER FOURTEEN

IT HAD taken every shred of every ounce of pulling rank that Rafe could find, every firm promise that the Beast of Iseo was a myth and that the weather was their worst enemy, but finally he'd convinced the *Guardia Costiera* that he was going with them. Rain lashed his face, his hair was probably wetter than the sea right now, but he felt nothing. Nothing but this great yawning pit that had opened up inside him.

He'd sent her away. Damn well told her to get out, and she'd done exactly what he'd wanted.

What he'd thought he'd wanted.

He must have been insane! Cursed with some kind of madness, because right now the thing he wanted most in the world, the thing he wanted more than anything, was the one thing he'd told her he didn't want.

Her love.

Because that would mean she was alive.

How could he have let her go?

How could he have sent her into the darkness, crying and distressed? And the yawning hole in his gut snapped shut, catching him in the inescapable truth.

He was his father all over again.

Casting aside her love. Telling her it was unwanted. And

in trying to protect himself he'd damaged himself even more. By lashing out at the one person who could show him otherwise. Who could show him how to love.

Rafe looked from the boat, his eyes always on the slick black rock, searching out any detail, anything out of place. The plume of smoke was long gone, but if there had been smoke, then the helicopter must be there, somewhere. For now that was all he would focus on. And if the helicopter was there, then so too was Sienna.

He would find her. And then he would tell her what had been so glaringly obvious the moment he'd known she'd gone, that he wanted to change places with her and smash himself into the rock in her place.

He was such a fool.

The cruiser rounded the rock, the beams from its powerful lights doing the best job they could to cut through the rain and illuminate the shore, every eye on board not concentrating on keeping the boat from the rocks, but searching for any scrap of evidence of the helicopter's position.

And then there was a glint of white where there should be none, and a cry went up to launch a dinghy. Rafe pushed his way to the front. 'I'm going,' he said.

Strange that she should feel cold. The thought came from nowhere, a kind of hazy realization that it was summer, that she shouldn't feel cold. It was wrong.

Sienna tried to move, but something was pinning her in her seat, something that kept groaning and waking her up, when all she wanted to do was sleep. It groaned again, the sound vaguely human.

Randall.

He lay slumped against her, sharing the scent of his fresh kill, and she remembered where she was, a helicopter down on Iseo's Pyramid, and laughter bubbled out of some untapped place.

She'd landed a helicopter on Iseo's damned Pyramid with the ugliest landing in history. But they were alive! At least for now, until that damned Beast found them.

She reached a hand for the radio, but her wrist screamed out in pain and she pulled it back, sinking back once more into grateful oblivion.

Inch by inch, with one coastguard hanging over the edge to check for rocks that might slice the dinghy's shell to shreds, the boat had made it to the tiny sandy beach. To Rafe it had been an eternity. An eternity of waiting. An eternity of wondering.

And now that they were finally here, was it already too late?

His feet were amongst the first to splash into the water's edge, the waves still surging in, sucking at his calves with ferocity. But then he was running. Splashing through the shallows and running for the unnatural egg-shaped object, its blades angled askew, the lighting from torches showing how they'd decimated the shrubs and bushes as the chopper had come down.

He reached the passenger door a scant second before the man behind him. He pulled at the latch, heaved it with all his might when it wouldn't come, and wrenched it open.

And there she sat. Sleeping.

Pray God, she was sleeping!

'Sienna!'

Her eyelids flickered open with the play of torchlight on her face, and he breathed out a breath he hadn't realized he'd been holding. She looked up at him, confused. 'I knew the Beast would come,' she mumbled, before slipping back into unconsciousness.

A doctor pushed his way in front of him, and he gave him room, while another worked on the pilot alongside. Rafe stood back then, the angry sea sucking around his ankles, the shadow of the rock looming high above.

Oh, yes, if there was a Beast of Iseo, he was worthy of the title.

It was unsafe for everyone to move them from the Rock in the night, but they'd established there were no spinal injuries and they'd splinted Sienna's wrist, and now she lay on a stretcher in a tent, Rafe by her side, stroking her hair.

Deep in the night, the wind dropping as the storm dissipated, she woke up to the touch of him, and she stirred.

'You're here,' she murmured.

'Where else would I be?'

'But those rocks… You're crazy. You came through those rocks?'

'I came to find you. Do you think rocks were going to stop me?'

'I don't know. But I never expected anyone to come so late on such a night. I guess I should thank you for that. I suppose you told them that the future heirs of Montvelatte were at stake.'

He lifted up her good hand and pressed his lips to it. 'No. I told them that the jewel in Montvelatte's crown was at stake, and if they didn't find you, I would personally feed them to the Beast of Iseo, one by one.'

'You told them that?'

'My exact words.'

'But why?'

'Because I realized after you'd left that there are more important things than avoiding love. And then I heard you were missing, and that your helicopter had gone down, and I was afraid I'd never get the chance to tell you.'

'Tell me what?'

'That I love you, Sienna.' He smiled down at her and felt

his heart expand tenfold with the joy he saw reciprocated, even in a face shadowed in the low lamplight. 'And I am sorry for all the pain I caused you, all the assumptions I made, all the decisions I made without even considering you.'

'You're sorry for all of them?'

'I know,' he admitted, 'there were plenty of them. I'm sorry it took me so long to realize. Sorry I made you feel like you were trapped. Looking back, it should have been obvious to me. Even back after that one night in Paris, I was annoyed that events in Montvelatte had intervened, that I would not see you again.'

'You were? I thought it was these babies of ours you were after—your potential heirs.'

He smiled and nodded. 'They were an excuse, and a good one. But even back then I knew I wanted more of what you had to offer. I'm so sorry it's taken me so long to wake up, so sorry you had to go through all this.'

'It wasn't so bad. I kind of enjoyed being behind the joystick again.'

'I heard. The pilot said you'd saved his life. And I got to thinking, Montvelatte needs a helicopter pilot.'

'You don't even have a helicopter.'

'No, but if my refinancing plan works, we could have. And I'll need someone to fill the position. If you're not too busy to fly me around, that is.'

She smiled. 'I think I accept.'

'That's good. And I have one other favour, that I really have no right to ask.'

'What is it?'

'I'd like to celebrate my love for you by asking you to share my life for ever. Will you marry me, Sienna, and become my wife?'

She blinked up at him. 'You're actually asking me?'

'I'm asking you. Pleading with you if it comes to that. And if you don't want to get married, I'll even settle for that, so long as you promise to live in sin with me forever.'

'But then your children will be bastards, forever.'

'I don't care,' he said. 'It never did me any harm. So long as I can have you.'

And then he kissed her, and she knew forever would never be long enough.

EPILOGUE

SUNLIGHT poured through ancient stained glass windows, showering the congregation in puddles of fractured light. Organ music filled the cathedral, and the scent of fresh orange blossom filled the air as the tiny page boy and girl marched their slow march down the aisle.

Sienna waited at the head of the aisle, watching the procession, wondering how it would look if instead of waiting serenely until last, she skipped past her attendants and claimed her husband.

Not the way royals were supposed to behave in front of their own, but then she was only new at the job, and she still had a lot to learn.

Her soon to be sister-in-law, Marietta, gave her a final smile and squeeze of the hand, before she too set off down towards the altar. Where Prince Raphael of Montvelatte, her Rafe, stood waiting for her, tall, dark and utterly devastating.

She felt a flutter deep down inside her, touched one satin-gloved hand to her stomach, and knew with a woman's instinct that it was more than mere butterflies. She smiled. The day could not become more wonderful.

Or so she thought. Until minutes later, when she joined Rafe at the altar and changed her mind. There, with the eyes of the world watching, together they exchanged their vows, and she could not believe that anything would ever come close to that feeling.

'I love you,' he murmured, as he drew her to him for the bridal kiss that would seal their agreement and their future together. And, as he drew her deeper into the kiss, to the delight of the entire congregation, she knew it to be true, and that the Beast of Iseo had finally been tamed.

POSH DOCS

Dedicated, daring and devastatingly handsome—these doctors are guaranteed to raise your temperature!

The new collection by your favorite authors, available in May 2009:

Billionaire Doctor, Ordinary Nurse #53
by CAROL MARINELLI

Claimed by the Desert Prince #54
by MEREDITH WEBBER

The Millionaire Boss's Reluctant Mistress #55
by KATE HARDY

The Royal Doctor's Bride #56
by JESSICA MATTHEWS

Life is a game of power and pleasure.
And these men play to win!

THE RUTHLESS BILLIONAIRE'S VIRGIN

by *Susan Stephens*

Rescued by the elusive, scarred billionaire
Ethan Alexander, Savannah glimpses the
magnificence beneath the flaws and gives
Ethan's darkened heart the salvation only
an innocent in his bed can bring....

Book #2822

Available May 2009

Eight volumes in all to collect!

NIGHTS *of* PASSION

One night is never enough!

These guys know what they want and how they're going to get it!

UNTAMED BILLIONAIRE, UNDRESSED VIRGIN
by Anna Cleary

Inexperienced Sophy has fallen for dark and dangerous Connor O'Brien. Though the bad boy has vowed never to commit, after taking Sophy's innocence is he still able to walk away?

Book #2826

Available May 2009

Don't miss any of these hot stories, where sparky romance and sizzling passion are guaranteed!

www.eHarlequin.com

HP12826

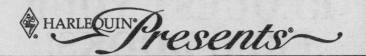

HARLEQUIN Presents

THE LEOPARDI BROTHERS

*Sicilian by name...scandalous,
scorching and seductive by nature!*

THE SICILIAN
BOSS'S MISTRESS
by Penny Jordan

When billionaire Alessandro Leopardi finds
Leonora piloting his private jet, he's outraged!
So he decides he'll take her for one night. But then
he realizes one night may not be enough....

Book #2819

Available May 2009

Look out for the final story
in this Penny Jordan trilogy,

THE SICILIAN'S BABY BARGAIN,
available in June.

www.eHarlequin.com

HPI2819

REQUEST YOUR FREE BOOKS!

HARLEQUIN *Presents*®

2 FREE NOVELS PLUS 2 FREE GIFTS!

PASSION GUARANTEED SEDUCTION

YES! Please send me 2 FREE Harlequin Presents® novels and my 2 FREE gifts (gifts are worth about $10). After receiving them, if I don't wish to receive any more books, I can return the shipping statement marked "cancel". If I don't cancel, I will receive 6 brand-new novels every month and be billed just $4.05 per book in the U.S. or $4.74 per book in Canada, plus 25¢ shipping and handling per book and applicable taxes, if any*. That's a savings of close to 15% off the cover price! I understand that accepting the 2 free books and gifts places me under no obligation to buy anything. I can always return a shipment and cancel at any time. Even if I never buy another book, the two free books and gifts are mine to keep forever.

106 HDN ERRW 306 HDN ERRL

Name _____ (PLEASE PRINT) _____

Address _____ Apt. # _____

City _____ State/Prov. _____ Zip/Postal Code _____

Signature (if under 18, a parent or guardian must sign)

Mail to the Harlequin Reader Service:
IN U.S.A.: P.O. Box 1867, Buffalo, NY 14240-1867
IN CANADA: P.O. Box 609, Fort Erie, Ontario L2A 5X3

Not valid to current subscribers of Harlequin Presents books.

Want to try two free books from another line?
Call 1-800-873-8635 or visit www.morefreebooks.com.

* Terms and prices subject to change without notice. N.Y. residents add applicable sales tax. Canadian residents will be charged applicable provincial taxes and GST. Offer not valid in Quebec. This offer is limited to one order per household. All orders subject to approval. Credit or debit balances in a customer's account(s) may be offset by any other outstanding balance owed by or to the customer. Please allow 4 to 6 weeks for delivery. Offer available while quantities last.

Your Privacy: Harlequin Books is committed to protecting your privacy. Our Privacy Policy is available online at www.eHarlequin.com or upon request from the Reader Service. From time to time we make our lists of customers available to reputable third parties who may have a product or service of interest to you. If you would prefer we not share your name and address, please check here. ☐

HP08R

You're invited to join our Tell Harlequin Reader Panel!

By joining our new reader panel you will:

- Receive Harlequin® books—they are FREE and yours to keep with no obligation to purchase anything!
- Participate in fun online surveys
- Exchange opinions and ideas with women just like you
- Have a say in our new book ideas and help us publish the best in women's fiction

In addition, you will have a chance to win great prizes and receive special gifts! See Web site for details. Some conditions apply. Space is limited.

To join, visit us at
www.TellHarlequin.com.